THE MAGIC of the GLITS

Other Avon Camelot Books by
C.S. Adler

GOOD-BYE PINK PIG

C.S. ADLER lives with her husband and three sons in Niskayuna, New York, where she was a middle-school English teacher for several years. She has been a full-time writer since the publication of her first book, THE MAGIC OF THE GLITS, which won both the William Allen White Award and the Golden Kite Award. Since then, more than fifteen books for young readers have been published, including *The Silver Coach, The Once-in-a-While Hero, Fly Free,* and *The Shell Lady's Daughter,* a 1983 Best Book for Young Adults. Several of Ms. Adler's books have also been published in England, Denmark, Germany, and Japan.

THE MAGIC of the GLITS

C.S. Adler

AN AVON CAMELOT BOOK

AVON BOOKS
A division of
The Hearst Corporation
105 Madison Avenue
New York, New York 10016

Published by arrangement with Macmillan Publishing Co., Inc.
Library of Congress Catalog Card Number: 78-12149
ISBN: 0-380-70403-X
RL: 4.8

The Macmillan edition contains the following Library of Congress Cataloging
in Publication Data:

Adler, C.S.
    The magic of the Glits.

    SUMMARY: Twelve-year-old Jeremy, spending the summer on Cape Cod,
befriends an eight-year-old girl whose mother has just died.
    [1. Friendship—Fiction]   I. Forberg, Ati.   II. Title.
PZ7.A26145Mag   [Fic]   78-12149

First Camelot Printing: July 1987

Printed in the U.S.A.

OPM   10   9   8   7   6   5   4   3   2   1

With love and gratitude
To my mother who always believed in me
My husband who supported me
My son Ken whose enthusiasm encouraged me
And my friend Cynthia Mendelsohn who
    gave me the criticism I needed

1

"Well, don't expect me to entertain her," Jeremy said immediately.

"Jeremy, how can you be so selfish? The poor little thing has just lost her mother. We have to be kind."

"You be kind." Jeremy scowled and stomped off on the cast that had already lead-weighted his summer.

"Jeremy!" his mother cried at him, her paintbrush an upended exclamation point. "I counted on you."

"Well, you had no right to. You invited her, Mother." He slammed the screen door behind him. Why not? She was always after him to close it. Angrily, he stabbed his crutches into the sandy path leading to the dune edge. There he stopped to brood over the softly breathing gray sea below and beyond him. She had no right to ask a twelve-year-old boy to entertain a five-year-old girl—well, seven-year-old this year—but even seven, a baby. Didn't she know anything? Just because his summer was ruined anyway with the broken leg, and now he couldn't bodysurf or build up his stamina by running on the beach as his gym teacher had suggested, and he couldn't dig clams with Keith and Kevin or do anything that was fun at all. He gritted his teeth. Baby-sitting was just what he needed to make everything perfect—perfectly rotten.

1

He couldn't even remember Lynette from that short visit two summers ago when she had come with her mother and Dave. All that stuck in his mind was his parents' surprise that their old friend Dave was getting married, and to a woman who already had a child. "Bachelor playboy to father in one jump; it just doesn't seem possible!" his mother kept saying. Why his parents found it funny, Jeremy didn't understand. Anyway, Lynette's mother was dead now. Too bad for the kid, but not—definitely not—his problem.

He reminded himself of that the next day as he ducked Dave's rabbit punch and said "Hi" to the kid politely. She didn't say "Hi" back. She stood beside Dave, a small, brown-haired waif with a curved-down mouth and eyes hiding behind her grassy thick lashes. It didn't look to Jeremy as if she'd grown at all since he last saw her snugged in beside her brown and gentle, seal-smooth mother. She and her mother had both been listeners. That hadn't changed either. Jeremy hated listeners. You never could tell what they were thinking inside their silence.

"You people are wonderful to take her for the summer for me," Dave said to Jeremy's mother, who smiled blankly in the sunlight and answered, "Don't worry about a thing, Dave. We'll have her eating again and perky as a chipmunk in no time."

"She misses her mother more than I do, if that's possible," Dave said. "It seems we both need a boost to get us back on our feet." He gave a faded imitation of his old grin. Lynette kept her eyes on her suitcase as if she were deaf. Even the sound of Dave's car starting didn't make her look up, though she rubbed impatiently at an eye that maybe was threatening to tear.

Dumb, just the way adults would figure it, Jeremy thought. She loses her mother, so her stepfather goes off and leaves her too, and they all expect her to feel great. He looked at his mother, who looked worried now that Dave had gone. In an artificially bright voice, his mother chirruped, "Lynette, why don't you change into your bathing suit, and Jeremy can show you where to play on the beach." She smiled encouragement at Lynette and challenged Jeremy to dare object all at the same time. His mother was good at these dual messages. Jeremy figured she was already thinking about how much light was left for her to paint with today. In a minute she'd disappear up into the attic where his father had installed a skylight so that she could work indoors all summer. That would leave Jeremy right where she'd intended to have him—in charge of Lynette.

"Mother," Jeremy said, "I have work to do in my room this afternoon. See you later." He swung his crutches in wide arcs of escape and rocked speedily off to his room, shutting the door firmly behind him.

All afternoon he labeled his shells, gluing them neatly onto weathered clapboard with the labels below each. At dinner Lynette was still hidden behind her curtain of hair. "She hasn't eaten anything," his mother hissed at him in the kitchen where he went to help her do the dishes. "And she wouldn't go to the beach at all. What am I going to do?"

Jeremy shrugged. "I don't know. You shouldn't of said you'd take care of her."

"How can you be so self-centered? Don't you care about anybody but yourself?"

He didn't care. It was like his mother to take on responsibilities and then try to slough them off on some-body else. He had plenty to handle this summer carting around a cast with enough white plaster in it to cover a whole ceiling.

3

2

The next day it rained. Lynette sat all day curled into a corner of the armchair, staring at the rain-spattered window, her face a blob of misery smooth as a raindrop. On Wednesday when the sun shone, Jeremy struggled into his baggiest bathing trunks. He couldn't swim or snorkel or run or bodysurf, but he could at least go look at the water. He clomped through the living room and stopped. There sat Lynette with her chin on her arms in the same armchair, still staring out the window. The stillness of her got to Jeremy. Without giving it much thought, he said, "Hey, come on down to the ocean with me."

Lynette's small, blank face turned his way.

"Come on," he said impatiently. "I haven't got all day."

She straightened up, thinking about it. He frowned. "Just a minute," she said and flew upstairs while he waited and cursed himself for being a sucker.

It was a perfect blue and gold beach day. He tied a plastic bag over his foot to cover the open-toed cast, and switched to the crutches specially rigged out with balsa wood pontoons so they would ride on the soft sand.

4

When Lynette came back in her bathing suit, he swung off, shoving his crutches viciously before him at the glistening beige sand. What good was the purling white edge of a blue-green sea when you had a cast that couldn't get wet? He glanced sideways to see if she was following. The wind flicked back her hair, and he was reminded suddenly of how pretty her mother had been— the small, brown-animal look, like a wood thrush or chipmunk. He had a secret soft spot for the quiet, small, woodsy creatures.

At the edge of the soft sand, where it broke off at the slope hard packed by the inrushing waves, he sat down with a sigh. Rotten to have to stop there. "Why don't you go in?" he said, his suggestion bitter-edged with self-pity. She squatted down on her heels beside him and shook her head.

"Why not?"

"I don't like the water."

Dumb, he scolded himself silently. He'd forgotten. Her mother had drowned on their winter vacation to Florida. Silently they sat side by side. It was sure going to be a wasted summer, he thought. Her fingers sifted through the warm sand, and the grains showered down— black, beige, crystalline white, yellow and red—so many colors if you looked close. He loved not only the feel, but the look of it.

"Want to build a sand castle?" he asked.

"O.K."

He scoonched down to the hard, damp sand leaving his crutches behind and began a mound with wide sweeps of his arms. She watched him, her chin resting on her knees.

"Aren't you going to help?" he asked. After all, the sand castle was for her entertainment. He was too old for that sort of thing. Obediently she crouched beside him and began to double-scoop the sand and pat it onto his pile. "Turrets," he said, "and a moat—sort of a Disney castle? Or do you want to try a walled city with little houses inside?"

She shrugged, and the down-turned mouth turned up. He felt proud of the smile. He'd produced it, even if she was laughing at him. He couldn't exactly tell. She was such a mysterious creature. "I specialize in creative castles," he joked, imitating some of his mother's arty friends. "What's your pleasure, madam?"

"A castle for fairies," she said breathlessly.

"Fairies!" He drew the word out with disgust. "You don't believe in *fairies,* do you?"

Her smile flinched and went out. She looked toward the vague horizon so that the wind blew brown veils of hair over her face. But he could tell by the droop of her narrow shoulders just how dead he had killed the smile.

"Come on," he said. "Over there's a paper cup someone left. I'll let you make the towers."

She kept drawing her fingers through the sand, making narrow ridges, but she did not move. What now, he thought, and wished he had not axed the fairies so hard. At seven maybe a little kid could still believe in fairies. That was the trouble. A boy his age was no fit companion for a little girl like Lynette, even if he wanted to take on the job. He got up and hobbled over to retrieve his crutches. He could call Keith and ask him to come over and fish or something. Keith liked to fish, though Jeremy thought waiting around all day just to catch something he did not like to eat anyway was stupid. He glanced back. Lynette was molding neat paper-cup towers on the top of the mound he had built.

He sighed. "Not that way, dummy."

She sat back on her heels and looked up at him. "Will you show me how?"

6

"O.K., all right," he said. "But then I've got things to do."

Together they built an elaborate castle with interior courtyards with four turreted towers around each. He poked in careful holes for doors and windows and neatly squared off the steps for a staircase from a courtyard up to the tower wall.

"There could be fairies," she ventured at the end of the afternoon when they were trudging back across the beach and up the dune to the weathered, gray-shingled cottage. He did not answer her. "If there were fairies," she said skipping along to keep up with him, "I expect they'd like that castle we built for them."

"That castle is for the Glits," he said firmly, unable to swallow the sugary stickiness of fairies. Then before she could ask him what Glits were, he told her he had a phone call to make and took off.

The next day it rained. Jeremy covered his cast with a plastic garbage bag and went fishing with Keith and Kevin. He had a rowdy good time and brought back a six-pound tautog. "The best thing was knocking Kevin off the bridge," he told his mother as she filleted the fish. "Boy, did he look funny!"

"Jeremy, I don't know what to do about Lynette," his mother said. "She wrote a letter and badgered me for a stamp until I found one. Then she sat in the armchair looking miserable all morning."

"Why don't you let her paint with you?"

"I did. She says she doesn't like to paint. Very emphatically. She may look like a kitten, but she's willful as a cat who knows what it likes. I can't reach her. I really can't. Shall I call Dave and say he'd better try summer camp after all?"

"Maybe."

7

"Dave said she doesn't make friends easily. I wonder how she'd take to singing around the campfire with strangers."

"Tomorrow Keith is coming over to work on my engine with me," he said. He knew his mother. She was digging for his sympathy and flattering him by taking him into her confidence. No way, Ma, he thought.

Keith didn't show the next day, and by noon Jeremy was tired of cleaning spark plugs and trying to time the engine. He slapped some salami on oatmeal bread for lunch and drifted along to the beach. He found Lynette down at the beach edge, not doing anything, just sifting sand through her fingers.

"Hi," he said.

She looked up without surprise. "The castle's gone."

"Natch. Sure. The tide came in. High tide comes twice a day, after all."

She didn't say anything. Her face was lost behind the hair again, and the rest of her was folded tight into herself. "Look," he said in exasperation. "It doesn't make sense to go around being sad forever. Your mother wouldn't like you to."

"What's a Glit, Jeremy?" It distracted him to see her eyes open to him as if he were someone she could trust.

"A Glit?" he asked, and then remembered. "A Glit—" he stalled for time. "It's hard to explain. They're creatures, you know, little—I think—I'm not sure because I've never seen one myself. I mean, you have to be a very good person to see one, and I'm not good."

"I think you're good."

"No, I'm not. Anyway, not good enough to see a Glit. See, you have to be pretty near perfect for that, and I'm no way perfect." He thought of his mother's frequent complaint that he was such a little male egotist.

8

"I'm self-centered, and besides, I've got a rotten mean temper."

"But are they like—you know—" She didn't want to irritate him, but he knew what she meant.

"Fairies? No. They're not. They're sort of not human-looking like a fairy. They're more—well, they live in sand-crab holes and they eat sea clams and seaweed and stuff. They're realer than fairies, you know?" He spoke positively, discarding the gooey nonsense of fairies once and for all.

She wrinkled her nose with distaste. "I think they're ugly. Glit is an ugly name."

He was hurt. "They are not ugly! See, what's special about them is that they have this magic power."

"Really?"

"Really. If you get touched by a Glit, then something special happens to you."

"What?"

"I don't know exactly."

"How do you know about Glits, Jeremy?"

"What?"

"About Glits. Are they in storybooks?"

"No, dummy. Fairies are in storybooks. Glits are real."

"Could we find one, do you think?"

"You might. I mean, you're a good girl, aren't you?"

She nodded. "Oh, yes. My mother said—" She swallowed on the soreness of that and then pushed on. "My mother said I am the best girl in the whole world."

Jeremy nodded. "You could probably find a Glit then."

"Where?"

"Oh, around. They hide mostly."

"In sand-crab holes?"

"Or in empty shells, or like today—look at the water." She looked with interest at the sequined waves. "They flash a lot, see? So on sunny days Glits can hide on the wave tips because you can't see them with the water sparkling too."

"Oh!"

"What they really like," he said, inspired as he'd never been when he chewed the end of his pencil in English class, "is when people build really neat sand castles for them, like we did the other day. They like to play in the sand castles when nobody's looking. They're dancing kinds of creatures—happy like."

"Yes," she said. "Can we build another sand castle then?"

"You build one," he said. "I've got things to do." Her sudden frown startled him into offering, "I'll come back later and check out what you've done, if you like."

She folded her arms and turned her back on him. "You're just getting rid of me, I know. There aren't any Glits. I'll bet there never was a Glit. You made them up because I'm a little girl, and you think you're such a big boy."

"Hey," he said, taken aback by her X-ray understanding. "Hey, that's not true. There are too Glits. I told you. Now if you don't want to believe me—"

She looked over her shoulder at him, and he marveled at the smoky power of her gaze. "I do believe you," she said, "if you stay and help me. Please, Jeremy!"

Such a strong appeal coming from such a sad, soft little girl confused him enough to make him give in. That day they built a sand castle so magnificent that passersby stopped to compliment it. One woman offered a sea-gull feather as decoration. Beach stones studded mosaic walls, and twigs and bits of straw made fences and gates. Tunnels and open runways threaded a maze of passages through the terraces and courtyards.

"How will we know if they liked it?" Lynette asked when they trudged back up to the cottage at Jeremy's mother's call to dinner.

"They'll probably leave a sign," Jeremy said.

"Will they really? What kind of a sign?"

"I don't know. We'll find out tomorrow."

3

The next day Jeremy woke to an itching leg. He cracked the cast a good one on the corner of his dresser, but it didn't help. He was filling up on leftover spaghetti when his mother walked in puffy-eyed under her tan and immediately began giving him trouble.

"Jeremy, you're disgusting. How can you sit there wolfing down cold spaghetti for breakfast? And did you shore up that mailbox like I asked you?"

"Not yet."

"Well, how about getting to it—like today?"

"I'll try."

"You're worse than the repairmen. At least they smile when they give me the run-around. How's Lynette?"

"How should I know?"

"She seems to be spending a lot of time with you."

He shrugged.

"She must like you. I can't imagine why. Can you get her to talk?"

"About what?"

"I don't know. anything. Dave wants to know how she is, and I don't have a clue."

"She's all right, I guess."

"Dave says he got in touch with her grandparents. They're French Canadians, and they don't speak English, so it's hard for him to communicate with them. But apparently they're claiming they're too old to take on a seven-year-old grandchild."

"Doesn't Dave want her?"

"I don't know. I suspect he feels sort of at a loss. What's he going to do with a little girl without a mother to take care of her?"

"Boy!" Jeremy exploded, standing up and clunking over to the sink with the empty plastic container and fork. "And you say *I'm* self-centered!"

A gray lid of clouds was squeezing down on the milky-white horizon. The dishwater-colored waves rolled in glassily and broke off in white froth. Five sandpipers twiddled along the edge of the surf on straw-stemmed legs. Lynette danced about asking what they were and then trying to get close to them, almost quick as a sandpiper herself, but not quite. She had come looking for Jeremy this morning, quickened with excitement. "Let's go, Jeremy. Let's see if they left a sign."

But he made her wait till he lashed the tripod of driftwood he had improvised to support the mailbox and nailed the box firmly in place. Even without sun, the beach was specked with people walking, hunting shells and rocks and whatever the sea might have left behind as the tide went out. He hoped no one had scavenged their sand castle since he'd gone early that morning to place the token. Lynette, giving up on the sandpipers, ran to the half-ruined remains of their tide-washed palace. He heard her delighted squeal and grinned to himself.

"Look, Jeremy! Look at what they left."

"What?" he asked, working the crutches laboriously in the sand.

13

"Shall I pick him up? Shall we throw him back? Can I keep him in a bowl? Hurry."

It was his turn to be surprised. He looked down into the bowl that was all that remained of the inner courtyard, and there was a four-inch-long silver fish. The sudden flap of its tail proved it was still alive.

"Isn't it pretty, Jeremy? Can I keep it? Do you think it would be happy in a bowl?"

"No." He shook his head. "It's got to have a saltwater aquarium with constantly circulating water. It wouldn't live, Lynette."

"Oh." They stood still for a minute, Lynette regretting her fish and Jeremy wondering at the coincidence of its being there.

"Pick it up by the tail and send it back where it belongs," Jeremy said. "Toss it out as far as you can."

Gingerly she pinched the slippery tail fins between her fingers and carried the fish, glittering like a polished knife blade, to the water. While she was busy, he bent and pocketed the handsome, white-bleached sand dollar he had placed in the tower early that morning. The Glits had provided their own sign. Well and good.

"Now," she said, having sent her fish on its way. "Shall we build another castle for them?"

"Not today." He wasn't in the mood for digging.

"But Jeremy!"

"There are other things they like that you could do for them."

"Like what?"

"Well—" He thought about it. "A Glit is a very fast creature, faster than a sandpiper or a fish in the water. That's how they got that fish for you. That's nothing for them—to catch a little fish like that."

"But they don't eat fish?"

14

"Oh, no, just things in shells."

She nodded. "And seaweed."

"Yes." He'd forgotten the seaweed. She had a good memory. He would have to be careful about what he told her. "Anyway, they like other creatures that are fast, like fish. Sometimes they race fish for fun—and sandpipers. Like if you could run along the edge of the waves without getting caught by them, like the sandpipers can—I mean right along the very edge—that would impress them."

"And then would I see one?"

"You might. It's hard to say just when they'd accept you as worthy. There are other things also that you'd have to do."

"Like what?"

"Like—skipping stones. How many times can you make a stone skip?"

She shook her head. "Not once."

"Oh, well, you'll probably have to learn then."

She moved close suddenly, put her arms around Jeremy and hugged him. He was so startled he didn't push her away, and after the quick hug she slipped her hand in his confidently. "You'll teach me, won't you?" she said.

"How do you know I know how?"

"You know everything mostly."

He gave an embarrassed grunt and wondered how Dave could resist such a cute kid. "Lynette, do you like Dave?"

"Uh huh."

"I mean, is he nice to you?"

"Uh huh."

"Well, do you talk to him much?"

"When I have something to say."

"You talked to your mother, though."

15

"Yes. Mommy told me stories—like you do. Mommy and I always talked, and we played games together and we read books all the time."

"But you didn't do those things with Dave?"

"Dave's not home. Then mostly when he was home, Mommy would be with him, and I'd stay in my room or play outside."

Jeremy sighed. Problems. What would happen to Lynette? "Maybe when Dave comes to visit you, you ought to talk to him, I mean, *really* talk," he said.

"I like to talk to *you*, Jeremy."

"But the thing is, see—he's your father, but maybe he doesn't know you right. You know what I mean?" He looked at her puzzled face. How could she know? She was only a baby. She looked away from him, out at the water, and he saw the pretty profile again, miniature of her mother. A gull settled neatly on the water and sat as complacently on the heaving waves as if on a rocking chair, its white head up and yellow beak arrogantly sharp. The sun slid a beam of light through a crack in the terrace of fat gray clouds overhead.

"What kind of stone?" Lynette held out three for Jeremy to choose from.

"No, dummy," he said wearily. "They have to be flat. Here, I'll show you." His flat, kite-shaped gray stone, the size of the palm of Lynette's hand, skipped five times. "Rats," he said. "I'm out of practice." The next two he tried skipped the surface of the water four and six times respectively.

"I can make it up to ten sometimes," Jeremy boasted.

"You're so smart, Jeremy!" Lynette's eyes shone with admiration.

"No, I'm not. Skipping stones is nothing. You can do it too. In fact, you'll have to learn if you want to please the Glits." He showed her how to hold a stone

16

parallel to the water with her forefinger controlling its cutting edge and to flick it out just so; but the most she could manage that day was one skip. She was better at skimming the foam edge of the waves as they raced up the beach. "Tomorrow," he said, "we'll practice some more."

4

Jeremy's logical mind was trying hard to make sense of the things that were happening on the beach. Mysterious little things, each of which could be explained all right, but considered all together, they were strange. Like the way they kept finding small objects in the sand structures they built, more wisely now just beyond the reach of the high tide. There, even the strongest waves could only attack their walls for an hour or less twice a day which meant the buildings lasted longer, sometimes needing only a little repair. But often when they went to inspect a conical village or a simple single tower with a spiral staircase, they found a gift for Lynette—a barrette one day with a white plastic bow that she promptly used to pin back the silky hair that kept blowing in her face. Another day it was a pearl button, and then a sea-gull feather and a pair of angel wings, a shell that rarely appeared on any beach on the Cape and never, that Jeremy could remember, on an ocean beach. He couldn't understand it—the Glits, of course. But he had thought that the Glits were creatures invented out of his own head for Lynette's sake. Now he didn't know quite so surely that they were make-believe. In all the summers he'd spent at the beach cottage, he'd never found so

18

many unlikely objects on the ocean side. The ocean beach at Wellfleet was swept so clean by the water that rocks and a few Atlantic sea clams, the black dried strings of wrack, and driftwood occasionally, were all you could find no matter how many miles of beach you walked each day. And odder yet was that the gifts left seemed deliberately chosen for a girl, a little girl like Lynette who would wear a barrette or a crackerjack-box gold ring like the one with the stone missing they found once. Jeremy fitted a rose quartz pebble in the open prongs of that ring, and Lynette wore it proudly for a week until the prongs broke.

Strange, strange coincidences—if they were coincidences. Because something else was different too. Jeremy kept feeling that something exciting was about to happen. The beach, which he had thought he knew so well, seemed as inviting to explore as an exotic land now. And Lynette was different. When she was alone with him on the beach, she shucked the reserve she still wore with his mother. On the beach Lynette was a laughing, teasing companion who danced about on her sandpiper-thin legs keeping him busy teaching her to skip rocks or tell her more and more about the Glits.

And that was another thing that puzzled him. How come that he who'd never been exactly known for his imagination, being more of a doer and problem solver, good at math, not creative stuff—how come he poured out Glit lore as soon as Lynette asked a question? He could almost believe that he was possessed by something that was using his tongue and its own will, Glits speaking through him. For sure, he couldn't have made up all that stuff he'd told Lynette. Like once she'd asked if there were boy Glits and girl Glits.

"Of course not," Jeremy said. "I told you Glits aren't like people. They don't have sexes, and they

don't have families. They're all one kind of thing.
They're all exactly equal. Nobody tells anybody else
what to do. They don't have to *do* anything. They just
are!''

"But Jeremy—"

"What?"

"Then how do they get to be if there's no mothers
and fathers?"

"They get to be from the sun. They come off sun
rays in flocks, like birds, but all formed and ready."

"And then?"

"Then what?"

"Do they die ever?"

He considered. "Yes," he said feeling a sadness
tugging at his belly. "They die at night in the dark when
the moon doesn't shine on the water."

"They only live one day?"

"Sometimes. Maybe more if there's a very bright
night." He wasn't really sure, never having stayed up
all night, if all light was inked out or not. Then something made him add, and it wasn't his own imagination
he felt sure, "But even one day is enough because what
they have is a joy fizz, kind of like when people get
indigestion and put those tablets in a glass of water, you
know?" She nodded. "Well, they have whole days of
joy fizz and nothing else."

"But Jeremy, if they're not human, then how can
they feel anything?"

She was so sharp for a little girl, he thought, and he
considered the question carefully. "Maybe feelings can
exist outside human beings. Animals have feelings. People say plants do too. Why not Glits?"

"Why not!" she said and squealed with delight as the
stone she skipped flipped across the water five times
before it sank. "Soon I'll see one," she said.

"Yes," he agreed. "Soon you will."

When he was able to discard the crutches, they took long walks along the beach. Some days they didn't talk about Glits at all. "No use today," Jeremy would say if the clouds were too mean and the sea was aluminum. "They'll have gone to the Indian Ocean or the China Sea today." But he didn't call his friends. In fact, he made excuses not to see them if they called him. Lynette and he would poke along the ever-changing edge of the water, watching the waves and the sky and talking. Lynette had a mind full of talking games.

"If you could have spaghetti or Chinese food or steak, which would you pick?"

"Steak," Jeremy said promptly.

"Spaghetti!" Lynette stated as if no other answer made sense, and then they'd argue until she tried another trio. "If you could have ice cream or chocolate cake or apple cobbler, which would you pick?"

"Chocolate cake."

"Oh, Jeremy, me too!" And the game would continue. Sometimes it was naming cloud creatures, and sometimes they played a game Lynette had learned from her mother.

"I say rose. What do you think of?"

"Thorn."

"I say kangaroo; think quick."

"Pouch."

"I say kitten."

"Cat."

"House," Lynette screeched.

"Car. Now you go—horse!"

"Gallop."

"Rider."

"Spurs."

"Eating."

21

"Cookies."

"Breakfast."

"Muffins."

"Why muffins?" Jeremy stopped to ask.

"Because muffins are cosy. Mother used to make them for Daddy and me long ago when I was little."

"You still are little."

"No, *really* little. When I was three or four, before Dave, when my real daddy still lived with us."

"You can't remember that long back."

"Oh yes, I can. I can remember everything."

"Did he die too, your real father?"

She did not answer right away. Then she said, "I don't know. He went away. Mommy said he went away. And we went to visit my uncle in New Mexico that time. I liked my uncle. He smelled of horses. I don't know why my daddy went away."

He had made her feel sad again. He wished himself mute for his clumsiness and picked up a tiny piece of driftwood in the shape of a snail to distract her. She stared at it.

"It's pretty, Jeremy. I'll keep it because it's a present from you, not from the Glits."

"Don't you want presents from the Glits anymore?"

"No," she said sorrowfully. "They're too hard. Even fairies would be easier to find than Glits."

"But you *will* find them, and soon. I'm sure of it."

"And if I do, then what will happen?"

"Then you'll get a joy fizz."

"That's all?"

"That's not enough?"

She laughed. "But I already get a joy fizz when I'm with you, and that's mostly all the time, isn't it?"

He blushed and got angry because it had been years

22

since anyone made him blush. "There's more to it than that."

"What then?"

"You can wish for something."

"And it will come true?" She sounded doubtful.

"Definitely. But you have to be careful what you wish for."

"Why?"

He sighed. He did not know why. And then, as seemed to happen all the time lately, he had a sudden revelation. Quite surely something was putting these ideas in his head, he thought, as he heard himself telling her a story he did not even know he knew. "Once there was a boy who was so good that the Glits used to dance all around him when he went swimming—like they fly around teasing the fish. This kid got to love swimming more and more because when the Glits danced around him, he felt so terrific, like he was close to having a joy fizz. Well, one day when the sun was really bright, a Glit crashed into him by accident, and whammo! He really got it—a full charge of joy. Well, he jumped half out of the water like a leaping fish does, and he said in his head, not even out loud, 'Oh boy, I wish I could swim forever and never have to get out of the water at all.' Right away in front of him he saw a path of shiny silver across the ocean as far as he could see. So he swam along it, and swam and swam forever until the sun sank and he drowned."

"Horrid Glits!" Lynette cried.

"No, it wasn't their fault. They felt bad too. It was just an accident sort of that his wish was such a dumb one, and of course he didn't know about Glits. You better think carefully about your wish and make sure that it's what you really want."

23

"They should have saved that boy. They could have, couldn't they?"

"Not really. See, they're limited creatures, and they can't do much except be themselves. It's like a cow stands around mooing and eating grass and giving milk. That's all it can do. I mean, you don't expect a cow to act like a watchdog, do you?"

"No."

"So you can't expect a Glit to be responsible for what happens when it gets mixed up with humans."

"There's always bad things, Jeremy."

"Yeah, but there's always good things too."

5

It was early in August when Lynette found the stumpy blue bottle. She set it down on the kitchen table while she and Jeremy got peanut-butter sandwiches together for lunch. Jeremy's mother came in to make herself some iced tea.

"Fancy that!" she said, "that's exactly the shade of blue I'm trying to capture on my seascape. May I borrow it, Lynette?"

"Uh huh," Lynette said, her mouth rimmed with milk. "You can keep it, too, if you like it." She smiled. "I have another piece of glass that's pretty. Would you like that too?"

"I'd like to see it," Jeremy's mother said. Immediately Lynette flew off upstairs to her room, which was opposite Jeremy's.

"Well, Jeremy," his mother said. "I think this is the first time I've had you alone since Lynette came, and that's over two weeks now."

"Huh?"

"Your shadow—she never leaves your side. I can't get over it. I would never have given you credit for being so patient with a kid like Lynette. She looks marvelous. You're obviously good for her.''

"Ummmm.''

"But aren't you getting bored spending your whole summer with a little kid?''

"Mother,'' Jeremy said. "What's going to happen with Lynette after the summer? Is it all set with Dave?''

"Is what all set?''

"Well, I mean, is he going to take care of her?''

"I don't know, dear. He's still unsettled and awfully gloomy from what your father says. He's coming up to Wellfleet for the last week of August. We'll find out what his plans are then.''

"About Lynette—''

His mother reached out and patted his cheek, something she had not done in a long time. "You've changed more than Lynette this summer, Jeremy. You haven't kicked anything at all recently. What's come over you?''

"Nothing. I'm getting older maybe.''

"Is that what it is?'' She laughed. "What will you do when the cast comes off next week? Will you start running around with Keith and Kevin and kicking things again?''

"I guess so. Listen, Mother—''

"What?'' She was smiling at him fondly.

"What's the deal with Lynette? What happened to her real father?''

"According to Dave, he deserted Lynette and her mother and just vanished. He left them in some miserable little town in Nevada without a penny to their name. I think he was a pilot or something like that; but apparently he couldn't hold a job for very long. Dave says he was such an unstable character that Lynette's better off if he never shows up again.''

"And she doesn't have any other relatives?"

"Well, those grandparents in Canada—"

"The ones that are too old."

"Umm."

"What about an uncle in New Mexico?"

"Is there one?"

"I don't know. Maybe."

"I'll ask Dave next time he calls."

"O.K. Say, Ma?" He tried to sound as casual as possible. "If Dave doesn't want Lynette, is there any chance we could—"

"No! None whatsoever." She stood up. "See all these gray hairs, my love? I've got two children in college and you still to go, and I'm not about to take in a little lost waif at my age and ruin the few good creative years I've got left. No, sir, not even if your father were willing to take on a responsibility that's not ours to begin with, and believe me, he's not."

Jeremy stood up too and picked up his empty milk glass. "She wouldn't be much trouble," he muttered.

"All children are trouble," his mother said; "not that they mean to be, just because parents have to be responsible for them." She broke off as Lynette came in and presented her silently with her entire collection of colored, sea-weathered bits of glass.

"Why, thank you, darling. These are just beautiful! I'll use them and return them to you at the end of the summer."

"They're for you," Lynette said. "To keep." She gave such a luminous smile that Jeremy's mother bent and kissed her.

That night Jeremy tossed on his bed brooding about what was going to happen to Lynette. Not even the windy sound of the waves sliding up the sand and back

27

soothed him, and the sight of the moon's glowing path on the black ocean only made him sadder. He thought of the boy who swam to the end of everything and drowned. Now why had he told Lynette that story? It even made him feel bad.

6

The next morning he woke up with a solution. Not that he'd gone to sleep with a problem, at least not one he was aware of. But now with the solution clear in his mind, he could recognize the problem. How to make Lynette so useful to Dave that he wouldn't think of her as trouble. His mother said all children were trouble. Probably that was how Dave felt, too. But number one, Dave didn't have a wife now, and number two, Dave loved a hot breakfast, and number three, he hated cooking his own. Jeremy had heard Dave saying half seriously that he only got married so he'd have a woman to cook him a hot breakfast in the morning. All those numbers added up to a way to save Lynette from the orphanage. Jeremy knew how mean orphanages were from seeing the movie *Oliver Twist* on television. He peg-legged it downstairs, zipping up his cutoffs as he went.

"Ma," Jeremy coaxed. "How about donating a little of your time to a good cause."

"What cause is that?"

"Helping Lynette the way only a good cook and great mother like you could."

"How?" She put down her coffee cup and gave him that radar-alert look that always made him nervous.

He hesitated, trying to figure out a maneuver that would get her to turn off the radar. "Well, it—like it would help you too when Dave comes."

"I'm listening." She sounded wary.

"I mean every girl should learn to cook, shouldn't she? And if you could teach Lynette how to make breakfast—"

"How would that help Lynette?"

"See, then *she* could make Dave's breakfast and you wouldn't have to bother."

"Dave gets his own."

"Yeah, but he hates to."

"And you see Lynette as some kind of little slavey to wait on master Dave's wishes? What kind of benefit do you expect her to get from that?"

"Ma, you don't understand."

"I understand perfectly. You know what your problem is, Jeremy? You need a sister your own age to teach you how wrong these persistent stereotypes you have of women's roles are. If Lynette were a boy, would you want me to teach *him* how to make Dave's breakfast?"

"Well, you taught me to cook—a little." He fought on gamely, knowing that he'd already lost World War III through his own stupidity.

"Then *you* teach Lynette." She smiled sweetly, stood up and stretched, a relaxed conqueror. "It's such a great morning. I think I'll paint outdoors for a change, maybe go into town and sketch the wild gingerbread house on the hill."

"Mother!" He continued resistance even in defeat.

"Yes, Jeremy?"

"You said I'm being a good kid lately."

"Yes, Jeremy."

"But you never do anything I ask you. What's the use of being good then?"

Her smile reset in lines of guilt. She bent quickly and kissed his left eyebrow. "I guess there isn't much percentage in it, is there? Tell you what. I'll take you and Lynette out to dinner on Friday."

"Big deal!"

"It's her birthday."

"Is it?"

"Uh huh."

"You going to get her a present?"

"I expect so. What shall I get?"

"I don't know."

"I thought a sweater maybe."

"Clothes! Yeech!"

"But Jeremy," she mocked him. "Don't you know little girls *like* clothes for their birthday?"

"Lynette doesn't."

"No? Then what shall I get her?"

"I don't know. A Frisbee maybe? Or a really neat kite. Or—I tell you what. Get her a float. I want to get her out in the water, and with a float maybe I could."

"A float it is."

"I can buy her a Frisbee from me, or a kite." He hiked back upstairs to count his savings, which were cached in an egg crate with the coins in separated compartments and the dollar bills lying on top.

By the time he got back downstairs again, his mother had gone, and Lynette was spooning up cold cereal and milk for breakfast. He decided to hitchhike down to the general store later for her present. What was most urgent now was teaching Lynette to cook. He wished his mother wasn't so touchy about women's place in society.

"Lynette, did your mother ever teach you how to fry eggs?"

"Nope."

"Did she ever teach you how to cook anything?"

31

"Nope. She let me stir sometimes. But I got tired standing on a chair so long."

"Rats."

"Do you know how to cook, Jeremy?"

"Well, I can make eggs."

"You can? Will you teach me?"

He untensed and filled up with pleasure. She was such an easy kid to get along with. "Sure," he said.

He couldn't find the small, cast-iron egg pan which his father had bought and instructed them never to wash or scour, only wipe clean with a paper towel. His father claimed eggs tasted better made in an iron pan that wasn't washed. The big, black, iron pan they used for fish was there though.

"I guess it doesn't matter much," Jeremy muttered and dragged it out. "First you grease the pan," he began, showing her how. "And you put your stove on medium." He rummaged around in the tightly packed refrigerator for a carton of eggs and finally found one hidden in the back. "Figures," he said.

"What, Jeremy? Is it O.K. if I kneel on a chair?"

If she didn't, her nose would be on a level with the top edge of the hot pan, not too safe a position for a nose, he figured. "O.K.," he said. "But first you better crack some eggs in a bowl. You don't want to get any shells in the pan."

She dragged the chair over to the sink and watched contentedly as he took a few practice runs. The first egg squished onto the counter. The second went into the bowl with too many shell fragments to fish out. "I guess I haven't cooked myself many eggs lately," he said. "I'm out of practice."

"May I try now?" Lynette asked politely. On the first try her deft fingers smartly cracked the egg in two. It plopped whole into the bowl.

"I guess girls just naturally—" Jeremy began, and then remembered his mother and tried again. "I guess I'm clumsier than you are."

"Mother showed me how to crack eggs," Lynette said. "I just never cooked any."

"Oh. Well, the rest is easy. The pan's hot, so you just plop 'em on in and wait till they're cooked."

"One side only?"

"Uh huh. Sunnyside up. I don't know how to turn them over too well."

"You sit down at the table, Jeremy, and I'll pretend I'm making you breakfast."

"O.K. I'll be Dave."

"And I'll be—" She stopped right on the brink of saying, "my mother." He could almost see her whiten under the tan.

"You be yourself," Jeremy said.

She dragged the chair over to the stove and got the last two of the half-dozen eggs that had been left neatly into the pan. "How long do they cook?"

"Till the edges get brown and nothing runs," Jeremy said.

While she kept her eyes on the eggs, leaning away from the hot grease spatter, Jeremy picked the comics out of the pile of old newspapers. He was rereading "Peanuts" when he heard Lynette scream. He looked up to see her perched on the chair with the heavy iron pan, sizzling hot from the stove, resting right on top of her knee. He leaped across the kitchen and grabbed the pan, swinging it into the sink, eggs and all.

Her tanned knee had a dark red cup-size burn. She whimpered. He cursed, wishing his mother were there. She wasn't. No one was but him, and Lynette was looking at him biting her lips in pain. He took a chance on a remedy he recalled from someplace, ice cubes in a

33

wet linen towel. By the time he had the ice cubes ready to apply, a white skin-blister dome had raised up over the burn.

"I didn't think the pan was so heavy," Lynette cried.

"I should have said. I didn't think you were going to try to pick it up." He got the old first-aid book from the bookshelves in the living room and looked up burns.

When his mother got back around noontime, she insisted on unbandaging Lynette's leg. Then she began clucking and fussing and oh-mying, making more noise than Lynette had through the whole accident. Jeremy explained gruffly what had happened.

"You let that child use *that* pan? Don't you have any brains, Jeremy? How could you be so irresponsible?"

He couldn't have been more shocked if she'd thrown the pan in question right at his head. He was hot with hurt and cold with indignation at one and the same time. Who had told him to teach Lynette how to cook? Who had to go running off to paint? How could she be so rotten unfair? He clamped his mouth shut, so furious that he was afraid he'd cry. Lynette looked at him and got hysterical. She began screaming at his mother.

"No, no, no! It wasn't Jeremy's fault. He wasn't even looking. I did it. I did it. I!"

By the time he escaped to his room, he had an awful headache. The weather outside matched the day's miseries he decided, half tumbling dark clouds with birds sliding off from under them in all directions and half radiant, sunlit corridors. He dropped onto his bed, and when he woke up, it was late afternoon.

"Jeremy?"

"Yes?" It was Lynette at the door. "Come in."

She looked as if something exciting had happened, something good.

"What's up?" he asked.

34

"Jeremy, I went down to the beach because of the bird we saw—the one who didn't fly away yesterday?"

"Yeah?"

"It was gone, but—"

"What?"

"I think I saw a Glit."

"You did? How? What happened?"

"Well, I looked over my shoulder—to see how far I'd come back up the hill going home because it was hurting a little—my knee. But it doesn't hurt now—much. So I looked down, and I saw it."

"What?"

"Well, I'm not sure. But it was shiny, like a piece of the sun had fallen onto the sand."

"And—"

"And that's all. Isn't that exciting?"

"Did it touch you?"

"No, I was too far away."

"Did you make a wish?"

"Oh. No. I forgot." She looked embarrassed. "I forgot to wish. But it doesn't matter."

"Of course it matters. You shouldn't forget things like that, Lynette. Even if it wasn't close, you shouldn't miss any opportunity." He couldn't quite bring himself to tell her about the orphanage. He couldn't stand even understanding about it himself.

She sat down on the end of the bed. "Are you feeling better?" she asked as if he'd been the one to get hurt.

"I'm fine," he said. "How about you? How's your knee feeling?"

"Pretty good."

"All right. Good. Now how about going away and leaving me alone for a while, huh?"

She went, quick as a crumb flicked off the table, and he knew he'd hurt her, but he didn't care. He'd had

35

enough of female company that day. He spent the evening immersed in the biography of Jackie Robinson that he'd been meaning to read all summer.

By morning he woke up feeling normal, which for him meant energetic and comfortable in the world. He got a ride over to the store and bought Lynette a birthday present, a green Frisbee that glowed in the dark.

"Do you think I really did see a Glit?" she asked him when they were limping down to the beach together in the afternoon.

"How should I know? It could have been just something shiny that reflected the sunlight."

"It could have been." She fell behind him and was quiet going down the dune, but when she found him waiting for her at the bottom she said, "You know, your mother really loves you, Jeremy."

"I know that."

"And she's really nice."

"Oh, she's O.K. But she should at least remember *she* was the one who told me to teach you to cook." He felt the hot bubble of anger burst out of him like a baby's burp and got the same relief.

"Well, now I can cook. In a smaller pan though," she said.

"Sure," he agreed, and forgave his mother. After all, she didn't have too many faults, and basically he liked her pretty well. If he wanted to bother explaining how unfair she'd been to him over Lynette's burn, she'd probably apologize—probably. It wasn't worth agonizing over. He let it out of his mind.

"Isn't it nice we both have wounded legs now," Lynette said.

"Don't be stupid," Jeremy told her.

7

Going out to eat was no big deal to Jeremy. He'd just as well his mother had made a chocolate birthday cake and had a steak cookout. But then it was Lynette's birthday, not his, and he supposed she was enjoying the weird-looking restaurant his mother chose to take them to. At least Lynette looked happy, happy and perky as if she felt everybody was noticing her because it was her birthday. Actually only two other tables besides theirs had people at them. What mostly filled the room was plants, hanging plants with fuzzy leaves and bug-sized leaves sprawling all over and plants with leaves like giant grass blades standing around in big containers. The plants on the slick, black-painted floor and the black and white paintings on the white walls made the place look like a cross between a greenhouse and a museum to Jeremy.

"Isn't this place charming!" his mother crowed.

"It's nice," Lynette agreed.

Jeremy avoided comment. Instead he read the menu, or tried to. Everything was in French—of course. Anything to make the customer uncomfortable. He bet himself the food would be as phony as the looks of the place. "Try the chicken, Jeremy," his mother suggested.

"Which is that?"

"I thought you were taking French in school." She was smiling, but he didn't like it.

" 'Pou-lay' is chicken," he said. When the waitress came, he just pointed. The fancy bunch of words turned out to be a chicken potpie and no better than the frozen kind, as he expected. By the time the food arrived, his mother seemed to be running short on topics of conversation. She'd asked about what Jeremy and Lynette did on the beach all day, told them about how Dave had been Jeremy's father's college roommate, told them about the progress of her paintings and the one-woman show she was planning when they got back to Boston in the fall, talked about Jeremy's cast coming off and asked what he was going to do then. He knew she was having to work awfully hard to keep the conversation going, but since he couldn't see the need for moving all those words around, he didn't try to help.

"Well," his mother said in between forkfuls of what looked like stringy stew with mushrooms, "you got a lot of mail today, Lynette. Who-all congratulated you on your birthday?"

Jeremy watched a plump black kitten swat at the corner of a tablecloth. He'd point the kitten out to Lynette when his mother left enough space for him to squeeze into the conversation. He wondered why silences seemed to make her nervous. He found them kind of restful himself.

". . . and Grandma and Grandpa sent me a doll from Martinique for my collection," Lynette was saying. "It has a funny hat on like a little scarf with . . ."

"What did Dave send you?" Jeremy interrupted, suddenly interested.

"Jeremy, don't be rude," his mother said.

"But I liked the presents *you* gave me best," Lynette

said to his mother, and then turned toward him. "Can we play with the Frisbee on the beach tomorrow, Jer?"

"Yeah. But what did Dave—?"

"Dave's not used to remembering birthdays," his mother said. "Maybe Lynette will get a card from him tomorrow—or something."

"You mean he *forgot* her birthday!" He was outraged.

"Jeremy, don't shout."

"I'm not shouting."

"You're raising your voice."

"There's nobody here."

"There certainly is—are people here besides us. Now behave yourself."

"I *am* behaving myself. How could Dave be rotten enough to forget Lynette's birthday?"

"He's not rotten!" Lynette protested. "He didn't forget my birthday, and even if he did, he didn't mean to."

"Lynette's right."

"No, she's not. Why do you always make excuses for him? I thought adults were supposed to be so big on responsibilities. He's an adult, isn't he?"

"Jeremy, you're out of control."

"I am not. I'm just mad, is all."

"And you're ruining Lynette's party."

"I am not."

"You are too, Jeremy," Lynette said.

He shut up. In fact none of them had much to say to each other through dessert, which was a birthday cake with a sparkler stuck in it instead of candles. His mother began singing "Happy Birthday," But Jeremy didn't join in, and she rushed the ending, acting as if she felt foolish singing all alone in the mostly empty restaurant. They had a long silent wait until the bill was presented and paid.

39

"The dessert was good," Jeremy said in the car. "Thanks, Mom."

"You're welcome."

"It was a lovely party," Lynette said. "Thank you very much."

"I'm glad you enjoyed it."

"I did. It was very nice of you to take me out on my birthday."

So much politeness made Jeremy squirm. The party hadn't felt right to him at all, kind of makeshift with too much artificial everything. Lynette deserved better for her eighth birthday.

When they got back to the cottage, Jeremy's mother put on one of her piano-playing tapes and went outside on the deck to smoke the two cigarettes she allowed herself in the evening. The cottage felt like the inside of a jack-o'-lantern with its flickering orange lights. Usually Jeremy relaxed with that glow, but tonight he felt as if the cast imprisoning his leg was binding him around his entire spirit. Nobody was even going to try to save Lynette except for him, and how was he supposed to make Dave keep her—the kind of guy who didn't even remember a kid's birthday. Or was there some other way? Maybe he could pressure his mother some more, offer to take over all the chores so that all she had to do was paint if she would only let Lynette come to live with them, or threaten to run away from home maybe. . . .

"Let's play Go Fish, Jeremy."

"What?"

"Let's play Go Fish."

"I don't want to play cards."

"I can play I Doubt It and Pig too."

"Go read a book instead. I have some thinking to do."

"But—"

40

"But what?"

"It's my birthday!"

"You already had your party. Leave me alone now."

He ran over her feelings thoughtlessly, too involved in his own mood to notice what he had cut down. Wearing the problem of what to do about her future like a pair of heavy-duty work boots, he trudged into the kitchen and poked through the catchall drawer for a pencil and paper. His father believed in making lists. "The list," his father had told him, "is the first step on the road to a solution of any problem." First Jeremy wrote down the problem—to keep Lynette out of the orphanage. Then he wrote down every bit of fallout from his brain that had anything to do with the problem: Dave, reponsibility (not much), Lynette (cute, not bad ever, doesn't eat much, smart, too young). He squeezed the bag of his thoughts some more, but all that came out was—income-tax deduction. By ten o'clock he had a mutilated pencil but nothing on the list that seemed very helpful. His mother claimed sleeping on it helped her solve problems with her paintings. He was sleepy enough to decide that was what he'd try next.

Yawning and with teary eyes, he climbed the stairs. A strip of light under Lynette's door made him stop and remember. He'd been pretty choppy with her considering it was her birthday. Maybe he ought to end the day sounding a little nicer.

"Lynette?" He rapped on her door. She didn't answer. He rapped again and then opened the door and looked in. Her bed showed the rumples of where her body had been, but she wasn't in either the bed or the room now. Where had the kid gotten to at this time of night? He checked his own room, and back downstairs the living room, bathroom, kitchen and his parents' room. Out on the deck, his mother had fallen asleep. He reached out to shake her awake to help him search, then decided he'd be better off finding Lynette himself rather than getting his mother all worked up and maybe getting himself blamed for making Lynette feel bad on her birthday. In an emergency his mother managed O.K., but her voice tended to get screechy, and she said a lot of things she didn't really mean. He circled around the cottage calling Lynette's name softly, sure she couldn't be off in the tangled jungle of pitch pine and scrub oak between the cottage and the main road. All at once he thought of the beach. That was where she was, of course. He started down the sand track for the top of the dune, reversed and hurried back to get the flashlight off the shelf in the living room.

The moon was a great white stone in a sky littered with stars that lit up nothing but themselves. Clouds scudded past the moon leaving no light at all for minutes at a time. Though he noticed, as he climbed down the front of the dune to the beach below, that even in the dark he could see the white caterpillar edge of the incoming waves. But it was too dark. Mist, he realized, feeling the chill of it rolling around him. A white edge ran up directly in his path, and his heart flipped up in his chest. How could it be so close? Why wasn't the ocean where it belonged? Could it get him somehow in the night? He pushed down his panic with the weight of reason. Of course, it was a spring tide, higher than usual, and the water was breaking over a hump in the low part of the beach and pouring into a packed-bottom basin where toddlers sailed boats and waded during the day sometimes.

Then he thought of Lynette. If his heart was pounding as the trailing wet fingers of the mist slipped around him, how was Lynette managing? She'd be terrified. The beach at night in the fog was a scary place. Too much could be waiting in the dark where you couldn't see—night things, creatures of the dark that maybe could see you. The soft thud of his feet against the sand and the soughing of the waves accompanied the sound of his breath as he hobbled, clumsy with the cast unbalancing him. His ears seemed nervously alert, listening for clues to orient him and for unidentifiable sounds amid all the sounds he knew.

Now the darkness angered him. It was the enemy hiding Lynette from him. Somewhere it had her imprisoned within its creeping dark veils within veils. He called her name again but without real hope that she would answer. Once he stumbled over something hard, reached down and felt the smooth surface of a sea-worn log. At least he could recognize it as something real. He kicked it and lumbered on. Suppose he didn't find her? Suddenly the moon disappeared behind the ghostly clouds. He felt something like a wet wing slap across his cheek and jumped back. Whatever it was flashed and veered off in the dark. "Please let me find her," he whispered, resisting the panic that was trying to capture him. Just then he saw the yellow licking flames of a fire on the beach. He headed that way, scaring himself as a wave crashed over the lip of soft sand and caught his foot in a shock of cold water. If she wasn't at the campfire, he'd lose control and start howling. He'd never find her in the dark. It was like searching around an alien planet where nothing worked as it was supposed to. In the dark he felt so helpless.

At first he thought the fire was deserted. Then he saw the small hump of a figure crouched beside it. From five feet away, he could see the figure was Lynette. The fears exploded inside him like a Fourth of July firecracker, leaving him blissfully empty.

"Lynette, what are you doing here?"

43

She didn't answer, didn't look up, didn't seem surprised to hear his voice. Beside her was a small disorderly pile of wood scraps, driftwood and broken boxes. It had been left by whoever had built the bonfire earlier in the evening, he suspected. She offered a small, flat piece of broken basket to the flames and let it drop to the red embers lying on the beach stones which formed the base of the fire. She seemed hypnotized by the flames licking at the edges of the wood. He said more gently, touching her arm, "Are you all right? Did something happen?"

She shook her head negatively.

"Why did you come down to the beach?" He waited. "Lynette, answer me." Now he crouched so that his face was on a level with hers. He made her look at him. He saw the tear-tracked face and the eyes lost in despair. "Lynette, please. Tell me what happened to you. Did it have to do with your birthday? Was it Dave? Was it me?" He shook her to get her attention.

"My mother came."

"What?"

"She came for me, but when I got out of bed, she went away, I couldn't reach her."

An eerie trickle went down his back. "You must of had a dream."

"No."

"Sure it was. It had to be a dream. Your mother's dead. You know she's dead."

"No."

He felt more chills of fear go through him. How was he going to get her out of this? What was he supposed to say? "Lynette, you're still dreaming. You *know* your mother's dead. She died last winter. She—"

"No!" She screamed it at him as if he was hateful.

He didn't know what to do. Her wild face in the

44

firelight, the ghostly mist and the groaning of the sea were all more than he could deal with at one time. In a panic, he shook her. "Lynette, it's me, Jeremy. Wake up now!"

At first she was rigid. Then she turned around and dug her sharp-boned little face into his shoulder. She shook with sobs. Jeremy didn't know how to stop them or even if he should try to. He just sat getting wet from her hot tears. Anxiously he waited. She felt fragile in his arms as if anything at all might break her. The flames sank away. Only the glowing red treasure heap of embers was left and the cold mist at his back and the sense of being in a land with no familiar landmarks in the dark. How could she not know her mother was dead? She had to know it.

"Lynette," he said as her weeping stopped. "You had a bad dream."

"No," she said, but in a resigned tone this time, "it was a good dream." She shuddered and looked at him for the first time in a normal way. "Let's go back Jeremy; I'm cold."

He took her hand rising and wavering, uncertain of how to start back. Then he realized that through it all he'd been clutching the unused flashlight. He looked with amazement at the flashlight in his hand unable to understand how he could have held it so long without knowing he had it. Then he flicked it on and played the cone of light around the beach from the water's edge as far to the dunes as it would reach. The cloud curtain swept aside again, revealing the bland white face of the moon. Magically the beach resumed its ordinary shape for Jeremy. He started off confidently with Lynette's hand grasped in his.

No wonder she wanted her mother badly enough to dream her up, he thought. Lynette was alone. All she had was Dave, and Dave did not even care about her enough to remember her birthday. He dug around in the unused storage of religious knowledge he had collected from books and church-going grandparents. "It could be your mother's watching over you from heaven—maybe," he offered.

"Do you think so, Jeremy?"

"I don't know. It could be."

"Heaven's too far away." She said it so low he could not be sure he had heard right.

"What?"

"I'm lonely without my mother."

"Yeah," he said. "Well, you're not the only one anyway. Everybody feels lonely."

"Even you, Jer?"

"Well sure. Sometimes. Sometimes when I'm right in the house with my mother and father I feel lonely."

"How?"

"Because—my mother goes around all filled up with her painting, and my father—my father doesn't even know who I am. He thinks I'm this great athlete or something. That's how he explains me because I don't like music and books like him. See my brother, he's 'The Conservationist,' and my sister, she's 'The Music Teacher,' and he can talk to them a little because they're grown up, and he knows their kind of stuff, but he doesn't even try to talk to me. I'm 'The Athlete'—he thinks."

"But you are an athlete, Jeremy."

"I can do track pretty good. That doesn't make me a jock. And if I was even—that wouldn't *matter* to him. Like I broke the school record in running the six-hundred when I was only in sixth grade, and it was a big thing in the school. So I told him, thinking he'd be proud. So a week later, you know what he says to me? 'Jeremy,

46

your brother tells me you broke the school record for running. How come you didn't tell me?' " Jeremy looked down at Lynette, but he could not see her expression in the dark. "Do you know what I'm talking about, Lynette?"

"I think your father is a very nice man."

"Yeah, well you only know him from when he comes weekends. But yeah, he is pretty nice."

"I don't remember my father except a little around the edges."

"Around the edges?"

"Sometimes I think I remember."

He waited, but she had nothing more to add. He listened to the creak of the sand beneath their feet for a while, then he said, "About being lonely—you know, even my mother feels lonely sometimes. She says she does, anyway. Probably babies are the only ones that don't feel lonely because they don't know enough to."

"I don't like it."

"Nobody does much."

"But I don't like it, Jeremy."

"So? What can we do about it? You've got to live with it, just like now you know your mother's dead you're going to live with that, right?"

"Do I have to?"

"Sure you have to. What else is there?" She dragged at the end of his arm like a worn-out fish with the fight gone out of it. "Come on," he urged. "We're both too tired to make sense anymore. Let's get to our beds and worry about it tomorrow."

By the time they made it to the top of their own dune where it was lighter and more cheerful, in reach of the glow shed by the lights from the cottage, his eyelids were dragging with sleepiness.

47

"I'm not a little girl now," she said suddenly. "I'm eight years old."

"You're still a little girl," he said.

"But you care about me, don't you, Jeremy?"

"Go to bed," he said. "Tomorrow we have a lot of things to do."

"You do care about me, don't you?"

"No! I just go chasing after you in the dark for the fun of it," he scoffed.

"What do we have to do tomorrow?"

"Teach you to swim, for one thing. I'll make Mom take us to the bayside, and you can try out your float."

"Thank you for my birthday, Jeremy."

"You're welcome." She kissed his chin before he could think to pull back.

His mother had awakened, gone inside and turned the tapes off. They heard the toilet flush in the bathroom as they tiptoed upstairs and spun off to their own rooms. Jeremy shucked his clothes and slid into bed. Boy, he was tired. Tomorrow he had to figure out a way to save Lynette; but before he could begin to think about it, he was asleep.

8

"I wouldn't push her," his mother warned as Jeremy tossed the float and Frisbee and empty plastic bread bags for shell and rock collecting into the open hatchback. "She adores you so much I'm sure you can get her in the water; but suppose she panics. How are you going to get her out?"

"Don't worry about it."

"Well, I am worried about it. I think you ought to at least wait another couple of days till your cast is off."

"No. If she's drowning, I'm not going to worry about getting my cast wet."

"Oh? And how, Mr. Know-so-much, do you think you're going to get around in the water with a cast on your leg?"

"Mom, she isn't going to *be* more than three feet from shore. This is the *bayside,* remember? The water is so shallow you'd have a hard time *making* yourself drown."

"I'm as familiar with the bay as you are, and don't take that superior tone with me. If you think a minute, you'll realize you are rushing things unnecessarily."

"Look, today it's easy for you to drop us off and pick us up because it's right on your way to P-town, right?

49

And if I wait till after my cast comes off, who knows? You may not want to take us or the weather might turn bad. All I want to do today is get her to lie down on the float in the water. I mean, Mom—she's barely gotten the bottom of her feet wet this summer. If she's been up to her ankles in water, I haven't seen it."

"Sounds safe enough, I guess. Do be careful though, Jer. You're taking on a lot of responsibility, you know."

"I know. Don't worry about it."

"Seems to me I've heard you say that before." She reached over and tweaked his ear. "Don't I ever get a kiss?" she asked.

"Oh, Ma!" he exclaimed; but just to keep her agreeable, he gave her a quick kiss on the cheek.

Lynette came prancing out in her bathing suit with an old-fashioned, orange cotton, child-size life preserver Jeremy had told her to take along today. His mother sent her back for a couple of towels and a shirt in case the sun got too hot. "You too, Jeremy. It's wise to avoid too much sun."

"We're already tanned."

"Jeremy, don't argue. And I made you some sandwiches. They're probably still on the counter." She jingled her car keys and smiled pleasantly at him. He went back into the cottage grumbling under his breath. She sure knew how to milk a situation for everything it had.

His mother was on her way to Provincetown to help arrange a friend's art exhibit. Jeremy thought she looked pretty this morning with her hair loose and a white, billowy blouse with flowers in reds and blues and black embroidered around the neck and down the front. She looked like an artist, but a sweet-faced, happy one. He'd even told her she looked good. It had made her puff up all her feathers at him; she'd been that pleased.

Lynette was unusually silent as they drove through the empty woods around the ponds and out to the highway. They stopped at the gas station where Jeremy filled the red-white-and-blue-striped float with air while his mother got the gas tank filled. Lynette still hadn't said anything when Jeremy unloaded their gear in the parking lot, slammed down the hatchback and promised yet one more time to be careful. He waved his mother on her way and asked,

"How come you're so talkative?"

Lynette shrugged. He nodded, pretty sure he knew what her problem was.

"You take the towels and shirts and lunch, and I'll carry the other junk," he said, and set off up the path through the sharp-edged dune grass to the beach. He surveyed the usual congregation of people hampered by small children, beach umbrellas, chairs and coolers and picnic baskets. They always had too much to carry to go very far. A hundred feet from the parking lot in either direction you could find plenty of empty space except for a few fishermen spread out along the shore like fence posts. He never minded the fishermen, enjoyed watching them catch something in fact. He walked with Lynette trailing him, stopping when they got to a spot reasonably clear of straw and wrack and pebbles. Unlike the clean-swept ocean beach, the bay beach always looked storm-littered; but it wasn't the sand he was interested in today. He set the float down on the water's rocky-bottomed edge and said, "Come on. Try it out, why don't you?"

"I think I'll look for shells first."

"You won't find any now. Later, when the tide goes out. Most everything's covered now."

She pushed away some of the brittle strings of black, dried seaweed mixed in with pale dried straw which

51

matted the uppermost reach of the high tide and squatted down in the damp sand pretending to be very interested in what she could paw up there. "Look Jeremy, a shell!"

"It's only a jingle shell and you know it. Now come on, Lynette. You promised you'd get in the water."

"I did not promise."

"Well, what'd we bring the float for?"

"To sit on. I can sit on it right now on the beach."

"The whole point is to sit in the water. Look, you can ride it right over the rocks without hurting your feet, and you can sit on it without even getting wet."

"I will later."

"It's hot right now. I sure wish I could lie on the float in the water where it's nice and cool. If I didn't have to keep this old cast dry—"

"Let's play with the Frisbee."

He squinted at her, thinking, then flipped the float back up on the beach where it dropped with a hollow thump next to Lynette's cleared spot. "O.K. Remember now to flick the Frisbee like a skipping stone, almost."

They moved back toward the minidunes, pint-sized versions of the steep soaring sides of the ocean beach dunes. It was sandier back there. "The one who misses three times in a row is out," he said. He had a plan in mind.

They started off six feet apart, moved back a few more feet as the Frisbee went back and forth between them, and stopped when they began to miss the catch. If she suspected what he was up to, it wouldn't work. He had to go slowly. For half a dozen throws, he sailed the Frisbee right to her. She chortled with delight over her skill at catching. He kept missing, hampered by his cast somewhat and by her wild pitches even more. She won the first game. Then, cautiously, he began edging them closer to the water's edge so that when he finally flipped the Frisbee out into the water, it looked like an accident.

"You get it, Jeremy."

"You crazy? I'll get my cast wet."

She walked up to where her big toes got wet. He stopped behind her. "Go ahead. It's just a few feet. I'll hold your hand."

She took his hand, but she didn't budge farther into the water.

"Quick, or you'll lose it, Lynette."

She looked as if it puzzled her that her feet were motionless. "Jeremy, you get the Frisbee, please." She looked up at him in pained confusion.

"You want me to get my cast wet?"

"No. A stick!" The idea unfroze her, and she scuttled away from the water's edge and began darting back and forth until she found something that would do, a long, needleless pine branch which she handed to Jeremy breathlessly. "Pull it in, Jer. You can reach more."

For an instant he thought she had outwitted him, but quiet as the water looked, it had still managed to pull the floating Frisbee just beyond the combined reach of his arm and the stick. "I can't get it," he said.

"But it's my birthday present that you gave me!" she wailed as if disaster had struck.

He frowned. He had calculated right about the importance of the Frisbee to her, but not about the depth of the fear she had to overcome to get it back. "All right, all right. Stop bawling!" he shouted. He set the float at the edge of the water again, laid the half of his body with the cast belly down on it, and crawled the float out into the water with his good leg toeing against the rocks and the float keeping the cast up and dry. Once free of the shore, he wiggled farther onto the float and propelled it through the water with swimming motions of his

53

hands. He picked up the green, dish-shaped plastic, tucked it under his chin, one-arm-paddled around in a semicircle, and arm-rowed himself back to shore where Lynette stood waiting with a handful of knuckles crammed in her mouth.

"There," he said, pitching the Frisbee at her. He wriggled himself sideways and rolled off the float, still dry, onto the pebbly beach. "Look, I'm not even wet. Now you have to try it."

"No, thank you, Jeremy."

"You don't like the float?"

"It's nice, but I don't want to sit on it, not in the water." She had stepped back as if afraid he might grab her and force her onto the float. He could feel the fear vibrating from her like sound waves marring the gentleness of an otherwise gloriously perfect beach day. She looked at once so fragile and so scared that he couldn't help feeling sorry for her, sorry enough to begin to wonder if he was right to force her like this. Suppose instead of overcoming her fear of the water, she just lived with it. She could get along perfectly well, couldn't she, by avoiding the water? Why would that be so terrible? Plenty of people lived in Arizona and New Mexico and probably never learned to swim. Did you have to overcome fears? Why couldn't you just steer around them? He sat down to think it over.

"Do Glits ever come to the bayside, Jeremy?"

"Sure. They're watery creatures. They like the ocean best because it's more exciting with the waves and all, but you'll find them fooling around on the bay some days, too. They're probably out there right now."

"Do you think that was a Glit the other day, the one I saw from the hill by the cottage?"

"I doubt it."

"Why?"

"Well, I suspect, probably—" He knew it was cruel, but she had led him right to the idea herself. "I suspect that they're not likely to appear to a kid who's so chicken she won't even put her foot in the water. I mean even on the bayside where the water's just like a bathtub. I mean, you'd get into a *bathtub* of water, wouldn't you?"

"I'm *not* chicken!"

He had hit a nerve there. Good! "You're not? That's what you *say*. But you sure act as if you're chicken."

"I just don't feel like going in the water today."

"Or any day."

"I'm not chicken." Her lower lip was pouting up so far it practically hit her nose. She was really miffed.

"Well, it's good if you're not because Glits are brave and so full of life themselves that they wouldn't probably go near anybody who wasn't brave too."

"You said 'good.' "

"I said good what?"

"You said they liked people who were good."

"Yes, and brave too."

She turned her back on him. He just bet she was beginning to cry. "Wanna eat lunch now?" he asked.

"No." Boy, did she sound mad.

"What do you want to do then?"

"Nothing."

"I wish I could go for a swim. It's hot." He sighed deliberately. "Want to go wade in the water? So what if I get my cast wet anyway. It's coming off in a couple of days. Lynette?"

"What?"

"Are you too scared to even put your feet in the water?"

"I'm *not* scared."

"O.K. I guess you wouldn't mind then just showing me."

"How?"

"Hold my hand and we'll go in the water—just up to your knees. Not farther. Now that's not scary, is it?"

Her eyes were so huge with fear when they met his that he knew it was scary for her. "You won't let me go?"

"No. I'll hold on tight as a lock."

"O.K."

He stood up. She hesitated. Her narrow chest was bellowing in and out to the drumbeat of her fear. He didn't much like himself for what he was doing to her, but he'd already worked too hard getting her to this point to give up. Worth it or not, he wanted to go through with it, at least try it to see. Her fingers felt like bits of cold wire tightening into his hand. They walked to the edge of the bay. A foot more of wet sand had been exposed by the outgoing tide. He took one step forward into the water. Abruptly she twisted her hand free of his and bolted wildly toward the fifteen-foot-high dune, scrabbling up it on hands and feet and losing herself on the other side before he could even get himself together enough to start after her. By the time he got to the top of the dune, she was nowhere in sight. He yelled her name and looked anxiously toward the hollows choked with dune grass, bearberry, bayberry, lichens and poison ivy.

"Lynette, you come back here," he yelled. "Come on. It's O.K. I won't make you go into the water. It's okayyyyy!"

Finally it occurred to him to trace her footsteps in the sand. As far as he could follow them, they led toward the parking lot. He found her there hiding behind a car. She was crouched miserably on the blistering-hot, black asphalt. Grime streaks down her cheeks marked the tracks of her tears.

"Lynette, I'm sorry," he said. "I meant it for your own good. I guess I was wrong. I won't do that to you again, ever. I promise."

"I'll never see a Glit," she said woefully.

"Ah, come on! I didn't mean it. I was just trying to get you to go in the water. Glits don't care if you go in the water or not."

"Yes, they do too," she said fiercely. She got to her feet looking defeated.

"Come on. We'll find some shade and eat our lunch."

He felt about as mean as the kid he knew who used to blow frogs apart with firecrackers for fun. It had been a rotten day for both of them.

9

The doctor split the cast open with a round, whirring saw that sounded suspiciously like the chain saw highway workers use to cut down dead trees along the road. Jeremy held his breath, sitting very still so that the doctor would not have an excuse for cutting right on down through his skin and flesh.

"Did you ever miss and nick someone?" he asked as the plaster shell broke apart.

"Not more than once a week," the doctor joked.

Jeremy did not know if he thought it was funny, especially when he saw the leg all hairy and white and thin looking. "Is it going to be any good anymore?" he asked, not ready to accept the mismatched limb.

"Just give it a week or two. It'll be just as good as the other."

"But it doesn't look the same."

"Of course not. It's been an invalid for six weeks. Get it out and exercise it, and you'll see it come right back to normal. Don't worry about the hair. That'll even out too."

Reassured, Jeremy walked back to the waiting room where his mother and Lynette were sitting reading magazines. His leg felt peculiarly light but usable. "O.K.," he said. "I'm all done. We can go now."

Lynette clapped her hands. "Now we can go bicycle riding, right, Jer?"

"Right."

"Your redheaded twin friends just came through, Jeremy," his mother said, putting the magazine aside and standing up to go. "Their baby brother was having another treatment on his foot. They said they'd call when I told them you were getting your cast off."

"Oh, yeah? Boy, I haven't seen much of Keith or Kevin all summer. I wonder what they're up to."

He found out when they stopped in the candy shop to buy some homemade fudge. Kevin was there haggling over a dime's worth of licorice taffy which the girl did not want to sell him.

"Listen, I'm not supposed to sell that little. That's less than a quarter of a pound."

"But I don't have more than a dime, and what's the difference? It's all loose in the bin anyway." Kevin was trying his persistent nagging approach rather than the baby-blue-eyed-innocent approach he sometimes used. The girl probably knew him too well for the more effective blue-eyed-baby act.

"Listen, sonny, it isn't my fault. I just work here."

"Here, Kevin," Jeremy said, offering the quarter he had in his pocket. "Get a quarter of a pound."

Kevin smiled and slapped the money grandly down on the counter. "Jeremy, my pal. We missed you. Where you been hiding all summer?"

"In my cast. Where do you think? What's up?"

Kevin took the small bag of taffy, unwrapped one and popped it into his mouth, then offered the bag to Jeremy. One of the oddities about the twins was they ate constantly but stayed short and skinny, or as Keith preferred to put it, "wiry." "We're getting up a ball game at the field down by the docks. Want to play tomorrow?"

"Sure, but I don't know if Mom—I could bicycle over maybe, but it's pretty far."

"Don't worry about it. I'll have our mom swing by and pick you up. You still got your bat?"

"Sure."

"Bring it. We'll need it. We're playing some kids in the cottages down there by the beach. They claim to be some kind of hotshot champions."

"Jeremy, let's get going," his mother called.

"See you tomorrow," Jeremy said to Kevin. He followed Lynette and his mother out to the car feeling cheerful. The seats were hot and sandy. He sat studying his new-hatched leg with hope. It might look weird, but if it behaved halfway normal, it would be fine with him.

"Can I go with you tomorrow and watch?" Lynette asked.

"Sure. I guess. I don't see why not if there's room in the car," he said, concentrating more on his leg and how it would do in a softball game than on what he was saying.

"Where are you going tomorrow?" his mother asked as she swung the car past the post office and around into less trafficked streets. He told her about the ride to the ball game.

"I'm glad you're taking Lynette," she said, "because I wasn't planning on being home tomorrow, and she certainly can't stay home alone."

"I can take care of myself," Lynette said.

"Sure you can, but you're only eight, and that's not staying-home-alone-age yet."

"After dinner," he said, "you can pitch me some

balls, and I'll practice hitting on the beach. O.K., Lynette?''

"O.K.," she said happily.

They were just finishing breakfast the next morning when Jeremy heard the horn honk. He grabbed the bat and ball and his faded-blue baseball cap, and with Lynette at his heels ran out to the Ryans' old, outsized station wagon. It was roomy enough to accommodate six kids with an occasional pony-sized dog besides. Every summer the Ryans seemed to acquire a different dog—always a large one. Probably a small one could not survive a week in their energetic family. To Jeremy's disappointment the car was dogless this time.

"This is Lynette," Jeremy said. "Is it O.K. if she comes along, Mrs. Ryan?''

"Why sure. We can always pack one more sardine into this can, especially such a small sardine.'' She grinned a welcome at Lynette.

They scrambled in, slammed the door shut and set off, rattling, but secure. "This is Lynette," Jeremy said to the boys. "And this is Keith and this is Kevin. If you can't tell the difference between them, don't worry. Nobody much can.''

"You don't play softball, do you?" Keith asked Lynette.

"No.''

"Well, that's a relief. But then, why'd you bring her for, Jer?''

He had forgotten how the twins hated girls. "She's just going to watch," Jeremy said.

"Oh? Just what we need—an audience!''

"He thinks we're gonna be slaughtered," Kevin said. "I bet you they're not the great ball players they make themselves out to be. The thing is not to let them psyche us out.''

61

"Wanna bet they're no good? That big one said he was a Babe Ruth All Star, and besides they're all bigger than us."

"So what," Jeremy said. "It's only a game. We're just out to have fun, that's all."

"Yeah, but we don't need no audiences."

"I'll pick you up around noon," Mrs. Ryan said. "Have fun and behave yourselves."

"We can't do both, Mother," Kevin yelled after the car, but it was rattling too loudly for Mrs. Ryan to hear.

"Let's hit a few while we wait for them," Keith said.

Lynette sat down cross-legged on the grass just inside the backstop.

"She's gonna get hit if she sits there," Keith said.

"Move over there, Lynette," Jeremy ordered, and turned back to his friends. "Who's up first?"

"Why don't you?" Kevin said.

Eagerly Jeremy took a few practice swings. It felt so good to be doing something rhythmic with his arms and legs. He let the first ball pass and thwacked the second so hard it whizzed into the outfield fast enough to be a sure base hit.

"Yay, Jeremy!" Lynette jumped up clapping.

"Oh, so that's what you brought her for—your own private cheering section!"

"She asked to come," Jeremy said. "I didn't invite her."

"Does she tag along everywhere you go?"

"Most everywhere. We're taking care of her for the summer."

"Who's we? You and who else?"

"Me and my mother. Come on, guys. I thought we were going to play ball."

By midmorning Keith was in a nasty mood and Kevin was not much better. Neither of the twins was a good

62

loser. Nobody seemed to have taught them they were supposed to be. They did not even try to pretend. The big boys from the cottages across from the town beach were certainly good ball players, at least twice as good as the twins, Jeremy and the mixed batch of fill-in players they had patched onto each team. Lynette cheered loyally when any member of Jeremy's team ran or hit or caught the ball, but Keith did not stop teasing Jeremy.

"Hit one for your girl friend, Jeremy. Go on; give her a thrill." Or, "Run, Jeremy, your girl friend's watching." Needling was one of the twins' less likeable habits. Jeremy had never been the object of such a pincushionful of it before, though. It took all his fun in playing away. He would have quit and hitched home, but with Lynette in tow he did not dare take a chance.

At eleven a big-bellied man with knobby knees showing below his shorts called away two brothers on the opposite team to go fishing. By mutual consent that broke the game up. Kids wandered away in all directions without anything being said about playing again. "You know what?" Kevin said.

"What?"

"That was *bad*. That was maybe the rottenest ball game I ever played."

"Yeah, we lost," Keith said.

"I'm thirsty. Let's go over to the soft-ice-cream stand. Mom can find us there."

"Good idea."

They walked single file along the road toward the dock and lined up in front of the open window of the shack in the same order—Keith, then Kevin, then Jeremy, with Lynette a silent shadow in the rear. When it was Jeremy's turn, he ordered a coke for himself and asked quietly, "Do you have any money, Lynette?"

She shook her head negatively.

63

"What do you want? I'll pay."

"Just water, thank you, Jer."

He bought a coke for her too and handed it to her.

"Is that all you're going to get your girl friend? Boy, are you cheap!" Keith said, grinning.

"Shut up, Keith," Jeremy said.

"I think she's sort of young for him, Keith. Don't you think she's sort of young to be Jeremy's girl friend?"

"Why don't you stuff it, Kevin. Come on, lay off."

"He must be hard up, stuck up there in the dunes," Keith said.

"Look, guys, you're not funny anymore. Shut your mouths, both of you."

"Oh, listen to the big man talk! I guess he's showing off because his girl friend's here, don't you think, Kevin?"

"She's *not* my girl friend."

"She isn't? Then what's she doing hanging around you all summer?"

"She's—I'm baby-sitting her—that's all," Jeremy said.

"Baby-sitting?"

"Are you a baby, little girl?"

Lynette turned her back on Kevin.

"Hey, is Jeremy your baby-sitter?"

"Leave her alone," Jeremy commanded. He crumpled his cup and decided that he would probably get beaten trying to fight them both, but whatever the consequences, he was going to punch them both out. He whipped the cup into the swing-top, waste-disposal can and waited with his fist clenched for the next remark. He calculated how to get his back against a wall so that they could not take him from behind. A car horn honked.

"Boys, I'm over here," the twins' mother called. "I thought I'd find you here when you weren't at the ball field. Come on, hop in."

They all got in silently and sat burrowing into themselves, shoulder to shoulder in the back. Lynette was chewing on her lower lip. Jeremy was seething. He was mad at his friends, and he was mad at Lynette. If he had not had to drag her along, the game might have been fun, and he would not now be in danger of losing the only companions he had during the long summers in Wellfleet. As much as he loved the beach, it could get pretty boring, especially if he was going to have to be alone on it all the time. It was a shame that she was ruining everything for him.

"Thanks for the ride, Mrs. Ryan," Jeremy said as he got out.

"Thank you for taking me," Lynette echoed.

He nodded briefly toward the twins, not wanting to, but too well conditioned in politeness to quite bring himself to ignore them.

"Have fun with your girl friend," Keith singsonged.

"See ya," Kevin said.

"Rats," Jeremy said under his breath as the car backed down the driveway. When he turned around, Lynette was walking, proud as if she carried a heavy basket balanced on her head, toward the cottage. She went in and closed the screen door behind her with a snap. It occurred to him for the first time that she was mad at him.

10

Next morning when he made a casual circuit of the house, he did not find her. That made him angry, not that he did not find her, but that he was looking for her at all. After all, he was too old to be chasing after an eight-year-old baby girl to beg her to please play with him. If she ever wanted his company again, she could come find him. Meanwhile he had plenty to keep himself occupied. The question was, what? He kicked at a refinished oak rocker, setting it into nervous motion just as his mother walked through the living room with a pile of linens in her arms.

"At it again!"

Jeremy grunted. It made him feel better to kick things. She ought to understand that without needing it explained to her.

"Do you know where Lynette is?" she asked him.

"How should I know?"

"She said she was going down to the beach. But that was hours ago when you were still asleep. The big baseball game wear you out yesterday, old sleepyhead?"

"Must have."

"Grouchy, aren't you? Well, I guess one never sheds old personalities completely, does one?"

"I don't know what you're talking about. I think I'll go see if there's any berries still on the high bushes over by the ponds."

"Jer—"

"What?"

"What's the matter?"

"Nothing, Mother. What should be the matter?"

"Something is."

"Well, do you have time to listen or do you have to go paint?"

"I have time."

"O.K. It's like this. I just spent practically the whole summer baby-sitting a kid that's gonna get sent to an orphan asylum anyway. I lost my only friends on account of having her drag along, and now she's mad at me too. Otherwise everything's just great."

His mother laughed. "My, aren't we dramatic! Orphan asylum no less!"

"Mom!" Jeremy complained.

"No, you're right. I shouldn't make fun of you, Jer. You've stepped in too many mud puddles as is. Can I help in some way?"

"Yeah. *You* entertain Lynette from now on, and you see that she isn't shoved into some home for unwanted kids. Then I can concentrate on getting in shape for cross country."

"Dave's got to solve the problem of what to do with Lynette himself, Jeremy. I can't butt in and tell him what to do. As a matter of fact, I'm not really sure I know what he should do. There aren't any relatives who'd take her. That uncle you asked me to check out a while back turned out to be her father's brother, incidentally. The poor guy is scratching out a living on some would-be dude ranch, and he has more children of his own than he can afford to feed already. Maybe if Dave could put her in a private boarding school—if he could afford it—that might be a soution, but I don't know if he can afford it.''

"A *boarding* school? That's like an expensive orphanage, isn't it?''

"Well, hardly. Some of the best families send their kids—''

"Mom, the *best* families are the ones that raise their kids at home because they love them.''

She perched on the arm of a chair and looked him straight in the eyes. "Jeremy, do you think we have a good family?''

He sighed. "How did we get into this? I don't want to talk about this—not today. I'm already feeling rotten.''

"You mean, you don't think we have such a great family?''

"You're O.K., Mom. I mean, I like you a lot, and you're fun to talk to—sometimes—when you're not all involved with stuff I can't follow. And I guess you kind of like me. I mean, I'm your son, and you *have* to sort of.''

"No, I don't have to, but I do. I not only like you, I love you. . . . Jer?''

"What?''

"Maybe I should grab you and hug you once in a while so you'll know.''

"No. That's O.K. I'm not much for being hugged.''

"Well, how about right now. Give your old mother a hug so *I* don't feel rotten.''

He lumbered over grudgingly and shared a hug that was more lingering than he liked, but not too bad actually. "You know,'' she confided, "I know I'm basically not the mother type, and I do neglect you, and you are pretty much on your own, and I'm every bit as selfish as I accuse you of being, but Jer—I do adore you. I'm proud you turned out to be such a terrific kid.''

"Yeah." He pulled out of the embrace definitely uncomfortable with the flood of sentiment.

"And your father?"

"What?"

"How about the paternal side of the family? Are you satisfied?"

"What do you mean, satisfied? Do I have a choice?"

"No, I guess not. But—your dad isn't around much, and he doesn't like the same things you like, so you don't do much together. How do you feel about that?"

He wriggled, wishing the whole conversation was done and gone. "Dad's O.K. He's—he's never mean or anything. I just get the feeling he doesn't find me very interesting, you know?"

"Umm." She actually blushed, as if she were embarrassed about something. "Maybe as you get older. He's so preoccupied with his work and—but he's a very fine, decent man, Jer."

"Maybe I ought to talk to *him* about Lynette."

"Maybe. Maybe he could think of something or talk to Dave about it or—something. He'll be here this weekend. And of course, Dave's coming up in a week and a half."

"O.K. Maybe I'll just go down to the beach and make sure she's there before I take off."

"Good idea. And Jer?"

"What?"

"If Keith and Kevin aren't your friends anymore, you haven't lost much. I never could see what you saw in those two."

"They like to do the same things I like, sports and stuff."

"Maybe next summer you ought to go to camp. Would you like that for part of the summer at least?"

"Maybe. I don't know. Right now I've got other problems."

She laughed. "Yes, my darling, but I've no doubt you'll conquer them heroically."

Sometimes his mother talked really weird.

He hurled himself down the dune in three swooping leaps and had no trouble locating Lynette. She was building a sand castle on the sand where it was damp enough to make good building material, just above the retreating waves. He ambled over, studying her construction techniques critically as he went.

"That's pretty neat, dribbling the sand on that way. Who taught you that?" he asked, coming to rest beside her. Her building wasn't as solid as the structures they had built together, but while it wouldn't stand up to the waves at all, it certainly looked fancy. It was all spindly towers and lacy walls. Even Glits would have a hard time playing in it without knocking it down. He waited for an answer to his question. It did not come.

"Lynette? I like your sand castle. How long have you been working on it?"

She turned her back on him deliberately and began digging with one index finger a delicate furrow from the left corner tower to what looked like a moat.

"What are you mad at me about?"

She set four pieces of straw placed side by side across the moat as a bridge. He admired the care for detail but did not say anything.

"You could at least tell me. Whatever it is, I'm sorry."

"No, you're not."

"Well, I don't want you mad at me."

"You don't care."

"Yes, I do."

"No, you don't."

"Yes, I do."

"You're silly." She was really angry. She looked all drawn down and dark in the face.

"O.K.," he said. "It's up to you. You don't want to be friends anymore? It's up to you."

"We aren't friends," she said. "You think I'm a baby."

"I do not. What gives you an idea like that? I don't think of you as a baby, ever."

"That's what you told those boys."

"What?"

"You said you were just baby-sitting me."

"Oh, that!"

"Well?" She was so mad she deliberately squashed one of her towers.

"I didn't mean it the way you think."

"You told them—"

"I know what I told them. I just didn't want—I wanted to make them stop teasing me."

"Well, I don't care. I can play by myself. If you want to spend your time with them now your leg is all better, go ahead. I don't care." She pitched a cigarette stub out of the sand castle.

"You sure are sensitive. Why can't I be friends with them and with you too?"

"You can, but you won't be."

"What do you mean?"

"They'll make fun of you."

He crouched down next to her. "I'm sorry, Lynette. I didn't mean to hurt your feelings. Now are you going to forgive me or not?"

"But Jeremy, I thought we were friends."

"We are friends."

71

"*I* would never tell anybody I was baby-sitting you."

He had to grin. The idea of her baby-sitting for him was so ridiculous. Luckily she did not see the grin. "I won't ever do like that again—I mean say things that I don't really mean about you."

She thought that over, head down, then said, "I like you so much, Jeremy."

"I like you too."

She released all her pent-up feelings in an enormous sigh. "Do you think the Glits will like *this* castle?"

"I'm sure they will." He got up restlessly. The sun was hot on his head, and the backs of his legs were sweaty from squatting. Despite the breeze off the ocean, he felt sticky. He yearned to throw himself into the surf. It would be his first chance this summer to hit the surf. But before that, he had some business to conclude.

"Lynette," he said, "when Dave comes, you've got to be sure you spend a lot of time with him."

"What for?"

"You could show him where the swallows nest in the cliff maybe, if he's interested that is. You could challenge him to a stone-skipping contest. You're pretty good at that now."

"Am I really?"

"Well—good enough. Of course, maybe he doesn't like games. My father doesn't. He just likes to lie in the sun or read at the beach. Sometimes he fishes. Maybe Dave would take you fishing."

"Jeremy—" she curled her hand inside his until he took hold of hers. "Why do you worry about Dave so much? We have lots else to do with exercising your leg and finding stuff for our collections and looking for Glits. Dave will have fun all by himself."

"You don't understand, Lynette." He scowled at the sea, which was olive green today, so clear you could see the sand beneath the water right out to where it dropped off blue-black and deep. The frilled waves curled in like petals off an enormous flat flower, and there were enough whitecaps farther out for a million Glits to hide in. From the pale blue sky of the horizon, the sky shaded imperceptibly to sapphire overhead. Two kites, one red and the other a bright yellow, blossomed vividly against the field of blue, and the only sound was the light breathing of the breeze and the rush of the waves as the ocean breathed in and out.

"Lynette, listen. I can't explain why, but it's very important that you be nice to Dave when he comes. I mean you have to spend a lot of time with him and talk to him, talk to him a *lot*, the way you do with me."

She squeezed his hand. "It won't help."

"What won't help?"

"Don't let's talk about Dave. Let's make flags for the sand castle for the Glits, shall we?"

"Not now. I'm going in for a swim first now. You make up a good wish yet?"

"Uh huh."

"You sure now? An important wish?"

"Yes."

"Gonna tell me what it is?"

"I don't think so."

"Why not?"

"Because it's private."

"Oh, boy!" he chortled. "You're really something, you are. Private! I thought we were friends, and here you go having secrets from me, just like we barely knew each other."

"You can be friends and still not tell each other everything," she assured him.

He grinned and poked a toe at the water. One thing about Lynette, she knew her own mind even if she was

73

only eight. But even so, he could not tell her what was worrying him. He did not want to scare her: Lynette, if you cannot make Dave love you, you will get sent to an orphan asylum. He shuddered at the thought of Lynette in a bare barracks of a room on a cot lined up with a dozen other orphans and no one to care about her and somebody telling her what to do all the time. He remembered how Oliver Twist stood with his bowl in his hands asking for more gruel. She would die. It would be like when she first came this summer, and she would not eat.

He took two steps toward the green, slippery underside of an incoming wave and dove into it, barely noticing the shock of the chilly water. Swimming, he could use his arms, and the peculiar weakness of the healed leg did not hamper him. He stroked easily, heading straight out until he became aware of Lynette's frantic screaming. "What?" He turned in the water, floating on his back with his head up to see her.

She stood knee deep in the white froth of a broken wave with her arms stretched stiffly out toward him. What she was screaming over and over was his name. "Jeremy, Jeremy!" It scared him to see her standing alone that far into the water. In the ocean, the undertow tackled your legs as if you were involved in a football skirmish with it, and it was determined to bring you down. He began swimming back in a hurry to get to her before the ocean did. His arms pistoned against the heavy resistance of the surging waves. He fought the water for speed, using up his strength recklessly. As he propelled himself to the top of a good-sized breaker, he saw it happen. She went down on one knee and then went under. The turbulence of a shore-bound breaker had swept her off her feet just as he had feared. His arms and legs got a sudden charge of new strength. He pulled for the spot where she sank, feeling no emotion at all. All his concentration was going into driving his body as fast as he could force it to go and then faster. It was impossible that he shouldn't get to Lynette in time. It was impossible that he could. He forced his arms through the resisting water.

A brown splotch, too smooth to be seaweed, and a slender arm—he dove. His left arm hooked her inert body. He kicked to the surface, feeling as if his weak leg was hot-wired with pain. He gasped for air, turned so that her head was out of the water and sidestroked over the last wave. As it tipped over into the shallows, he got his footing in the tumbling rocks and dragged Lynette out of the water. He looked around for help, but except for a group of people just visible down where the beach parking lot was, and a man jogging down the beach in the opposite direction with his Irish setter running ahead of him, not a soul was around. It seemed unbelievable to him that a gentle sun could still be warming the toasty sands and terns could still be skimming just below a few contented white clouds while Lynette lay limp and half drowned. He screamed once for help in protest against the total indifference of people and nature. Nobody heard him. Then he got control of himself and started to think. What was he to do?

Gingerly he turned Lynette over and tried pushing down on her back to press out of her the water that she had probably swallowed. He would have been grateful to hand the job over to any adult, to anybody surer of artificial respiration techniques than he was. All he had to depend on were vaguely remembered notions from a Boy Scout manual on first aid. He pumped, feeling tight with anxiety. When her eyes opened, he was overcome with relief.

"Jeremy!"

"Are you all right?" He pulled her up into a sitting position. She sat dazed and covered with sand, and then she smiled radiantly.

"Oh, Jeremy, I thought you were going to swim out till you drowned like the boy the Glits touched."

"You could have drowned. You scared me so much, Lynette. Don't you ever do that again."

Her smile flipped over into a frown. "It was your fault!" she said and burst into tears. He waited sullenly until she stopped. He was now exhausted, and besides his leg ached.

"Come on," he said. "Let's go back to the cottage."

They walked very slowly. Lynette had the hiccups and kept shivering. Jeremy was irritated. Then little by little his spirits lifted. "Hey," he said. "You know what?"

"What?"

"We're both alive. Nothing happened to us really."

"Ummm."

"And besides, you went into the water all by yourself. You're not chicken anymore."

"I thought you were going to drown," she said and hiccupped.

"Well," he said, "I forgive you if you forgive me."

She took his hand then in quick affection. The sun, which had been momentarily blocked by a puff of cloud, reappeared. Suddenly Lynette squealed. She started up on tiptoe. "Jeremy!"

"What? What now?"

"There—don't you see it?"

And for a second he thought he did.

"It was silver. It touched me," she said in an awestruck whisper. The hiccups stopped.

"How do you feel? Do you feel anything?"

"Oh, yes! I feel it all over." She raised her sandy arms to the blue sky. "I feel fizzy with joy."

"It was too bright to see," he said uncertainly.

"I saw it," she insisted. "It was dark at the center when it passed, and it was bent like a—like a spoon that got bent—like a bow thick at one end."

"Did you make a wish?" She looked at him blankly. He felt the aura still around them. "Hurry up. Wish!"

She closed her eyes and concentrated into herself. "O.K.," she said when she opened her eyes again. They beamed at one another. "It was big. I didn't imagine that they'd be so big, Jeremy. Did you get touched too?"

"No, of course not."

"Why not?"

"Because—I told you—I'm not good."

"Oh, you dummy," she said. "There's nobody better than you in the whole world."

He laughed. "Dummy, what do you know?"

"Everything," she laughed. "I was touched by a Glit."

"Yes, you're special now."

It was funny how much better he felt now that she had her wish made. He only hoped she was careful to phrase it right. It would be a relief when Dave came and it was really settled.

11

The touch of the Glits had left Lynette with a curious sparkle. Even Jeremy's father noticed it when he came. He commented that Lynette was looking very happy, and Jeremy's mother answered, "She is, isn't she? I guess you don't notice change when it's happening around you daily a little at a time—although, I don't know, it did seem to happen all at once."

Jeremy evaded the issue when his mother asked him if anything special had happened. He didn't want to mention the Glits because he was sure they would think he was mentally ill or something to be believing in such creatures. And he certainly was not about to tell his parents Lynette had nearly drowned. He cautioned her to say nothing even though she wanted very much to tell everybody how he saved her. "No way," he said. "All that would do is make them crack down on us and make all kinds of rules about being on the beach alone and not going in the water without an adult around. What they don't know won't hurt them."

She agreed reluctantly. She was agreeing to most everything he said lately. When they were deposited at the bayside by Jeremy's mother, Jeremy marveled at how Lynette would splash right in. She would stand in water up to her waist and squeal, "Look at me, Jeremy. Look, I'm swimming!" With her feet on the firm bottom and her head cocked absurdly back away from the water she would make what she considered to be proper swimming motions with her hands.

"You're a great swimmer, you are," he agreed half mocking and half agreeing.

"Well I *am*, aren't I?" She bobbed out of the water to face him, demanding serious approval. "I'm *almost* swimming."

"Yes, you are."

She glowed with pride. He had the answer to the question he asked himself on the bay beach a week before, he thought, as she ran back to dance at the water's edge. How much was it worth to overcome fears? A whole lot. It was like muscle building. You had to go through a lot of pain and boring exercises, but then you had the muscles, and it was worth it in the end. She had a confidence now she never had before. He felt secretly proud of himself because he knew he had caused the change in her. It was his achievement as well as hers.

With Jeremy's leg out of the cast, the days filled with a variety of physical activities. He swam regularly in the ocean in the morning. Lynette would run in a short way and race back out with the waves yapping at her heels. The daily swimming built up Jeremy's strength rapidly so that he and Lynette biked over to Gull Pond a couple of times. There they played as many water games as Jeremy could think of, all designed to get Lynette feeling comfortable in the water. He wanted to begin swimming lessons for her, but the only way he could get her from a verticle to a horizontal position in the water was to hold her up and swear he would not let go. They sailed kites over the ocean beach; they raced up and down the dunes, and once they went clam digging.

It was the Sunday morning before his father was due to return to Boston and the business that consumed most of his time and attention. Jeremy reminded his mother that he wanted to ask his father's advice about Lynette.

"He's down on the beach surf casting. Why don't you go on down?" she said.

The sky had a gloomy gray raincoat on. The air was so chilly Jeremy had put on a jacket without being reminded. Except for the hardy surf casters and a couple walking down the beach wearing raggedy World War II army jackets, the beach was empty. Jeremy's father was posted at the water's edge, his baggy dungarees rolled up to the knees, his pipe clamped in the corner of his mouth, and his shapeless fishing hat pulled low on his forehead. He made a cast, starting the rod back behind his head and whipping it forward so the strong, weighted line would whizz out to hit the waves of the incoming tide just right. Jeremy thought it was a stupid sport. The tide was always turning at odd hours of the day or night, and catching anything in it was a rare event. Once two years ago his father had caught a ten-pound blue. He still talked about that. Since then a few flounder were all he had to show for his hours of patience.

"Hi, Dad. How's it going?"

"Jeremy! You up this early?"

"Yeah. Anything biting?"

"Nothing much." His father grinned. He always looked happiest when he was fishing. Jeremy could not understand why, since he was so rarely successful, but then he did not understand much about his father's ways. Last year in school they had offered a course during options time in how to play chess. He took it because he knew his father liked to play with his big brother sometimes. But when he got out the chessboard one Sunday afternoon, his father said, "Not today, Jeremy." And when they finally did get to play one evening because his mother reminded his father about it, Jeremy could see his father was bored. Jeremy just was not good enough. So it had not been much fun for either of them. But if he asked his father a factual question, that usually came out O.K. His father was comfortable giving out information, probably because that was like what he did in the government bureau where he worked.

"Can I talk to you about something, Dad?" Jeremy began finally.

"Sure, son. What's on your mind?"

"I'm worried about Lynette."

"What about? She's looking pretty good lately."

"About what's going to happen to her after this summer."

"Dave's the one has to decide that."

"Yeah, she's his kid."

"Well, not legally. He doesn't really have to accept any responsibility for her if he doesn't want to."

"But he'll want to, won't he, Dad?"

"Oh, I don't know. He's a good-hearted fellow, and he seemed pretty devoted to Lynette's mother. On the other hand, he's used to being free to do as he pleases, and he likes to travel light. The responsibilities of fatherhood would be a pretty heavy burden for him to assume voluntarily."

"But he *is* responsible."

"How? You mean in a moral sense? I'm not sure. He may feel a temporary responsibility until he can find someone to take her off his hands."

"You mean like in a store with junk that nobody wants to buy?"

Jeremy's father laughed, not noticing the bitterness in his son's voice. "Something like that."

"But Dad, how can anyone not be responsible when a kid like Lynette needs help?"

His father looked at him closely, drew the pipe out of his mouth to relight it, and set the end of the rod in the holder in the sand. "Your feeling is noble, Jer. But from a practical point of view, people simply can't take in every stray that comes their way. You'd end up with a houseful of strays and no life of your own. You have to limit your responsibilities to what you can handle. And the rest is taken care of by organizations set up and supported by the whole society—welfare and charity."

Jeremy prickled with indignation. "Well," he threatened, "if it ends up that Lynette's going to an orphan asylum, then I'm going with her."

"You are?" His father's amused look made Jeremy angrier.

"Or better yet, she could take my place, and you'd still have only one kid to take care of. I could make it O.K. in an orphan asylum so long as they give me enough to eat."

Now his father laughed aloud as if Jeremy had said something funny. "I think your information on social institutions has to be out of date. Have you been reading Dickens this summer—*Oliver Twist* or something?"

Jeremy shook his head negatively, keeping his lips pressed tight shut on his temper. His father knew he never read books that were not true if he could help it. Or he would know if only he paid attention to what Jeremy was really like instead of assuming he knew it all already. Sighing, Jeremy made one more try at explaining himself to his father. "I'm not much of a reader, Dad, except if I need to find out stuff."

"No," his father said. "You're more of a doer than a reader. And that's not such a bad thing after all, so long as you're a good doer." He grinned as if he had said something funny. Jeremy frowned, not getting the joke.

"Well," his father said, "as far as trading you off

with Lynette, let's get one thing straight. You are my son. You are not an interchangeable commodity with any other child.''

"Then how about if Lynette just—I mean, she could be a part of our family without your hardly even knowing the difference. She's such a good kid. She could help even.''

"Sorry, Jeremy. She's a nice little girl, and I sympathize with your concern for her, but your mother and I have plans that don't include being tied down by kids the rest of our lives.''

"What plans?''

"Oh, like after you go off to college or become self supporting, we'll move into an apartment in the city where we can take in the concerts, and your mother can get to the art galleries. And maybe—look, Dave's going to make a reasonable arrangement. Relax. Lynette's not going to wind up living on bread and water.''

The pipe was relit. The conversation was over. His father picked up his rod and sent the lure winging out toward the waves again. Jeremy opened his mouth and closed it. His father glanced at him as if to say, "you still here?'' Jeremy shrugged. "Guess I'll go back up,'' he said.

"See you later, son.''

On the way back to the cottage. Jeremy kicked viciously at a charred piece of driftwood, an empty bleach container and finally a rock half hidden in the sand. He kicked that so hard he stubbed his toe on it.

12

Jeremy looked Lynette over critically the day that Dave was due to arrive. The sun had turned her hair blond in streaks and her skin a coppery brown. He decided she looked appealing, more like an Indian princess than a small brown animal now. She smiled a lot and held herself proudly.

"Don't forget what I told you about being nice to Dave," Jeremy said, last-minute advice before he ran to answer his mother's call for help.

"Jeremy, get your stuff out of the closet so that Dave had some room."

"Well, where am I supposed to put it?"

"How should I know? Anywhere you can. Stick it in Lynette's room temporarily."

When he got downstairs, Lynette was sitting quietly on the wooden bench next to the fireplace, looking shy again.

"Hi there, sport," Dave said to him as he walked in. "How's the leg?"

"Fine."

His father was mixing drinks, and his mother was chunking up cheese which she asked Lynette to pass around. Lynette moved around the room silently offering the tray to everyone without being noticed.

"Going out for football when you get back to school?" Dave asked.

"Cross-country this fall, then basketball, then track in the spring," Jeremy said. "Doesn't Lynette look great?"

"I'll say, champ. You did a great job with her. Your mother tells me you spent a lot of time with her this summer. That was very nice of you."

Jeremy was stung. "That wasn't nothing." He began trying to get his tongue around a denial of time spent with Lynette as being a chore or a charity.

"Anything," his mother corrected auatomatically.

"What did you two kids find to do with each other all summer?" Jeremy's father asked.

"You tell them, Lynette," Jeremy commanded. Everyone looked at Lynette politely. She froze. "Come on, tell them about the stone-skipping."

"Jeremy can skip a stone ten times."

"No! *You*, what *you* do."

"Jeremy taught me how to skip a stone—once or twice," she piped in a swallowed voice. Everyone laughed genially, but that was not what Jeremy had in mind at all.

"She can skip a stone five or six times," he boasted.

"Well, that's great, Jeremy, a real accomplishment."

Jeremy glared at his father. All his father considered an accomplishment was some kind of scholastic success. Well, stone-skipping was important too, in its way. "Why don't you get your shell collection, Lynette, and show them all the ones you can name." He was desperate now, feeling foolish and sensing they were not really interested. Lynette hesitated, standing up to go, but looking at him for reprieve. "Go on," he insisted.

"Jeremy, what's the matter with you?" his mother

85

scolded gently when Lynette had run upstairs for the shell collection. "She's not a prize poodle, you know."

"Mother, you don't understand. It's just she's so shy. Once she gets talking, you'll see."

"See what, Jeremy?" His father sounded annoyed.

"What a great kid she is."

"We already know she's a great kid. She doesn't need to be sold."

He heaved one of his largest sighs as Lynette came back in the room with the shoe box of shells from the bayside and stood there waiting to see if anyone really wanted her to name them.

"Come on, honey," Dave called, uncrossing his legs and putting his drink down. "Let's see what you've got there." He held her in the crook of his arm and listened patiently while she went solemnly through her box picking up and naming.

"Moon shell, boat shell, razor clam, jingle shells, mussels, oyster, scallop, angel wings—" Jeremy was appeased seeing the way Dave's wavy-blond head bent close to Lynette's small sun-streaked one, the better to hear her barely audible voice.

The next morning when there was talk of a deep-sea-fishing excursion on one of the harbor boats, Jeremy asked if he and Lynette could go along.

"Oh, come on, Jer—you don't even like to fish," his father said, definitely annoyed now at Jeremy's unaccountable horning in.

"Lynette does."

"No, I don't."

Dave laughed. "Lynette's the most honest little girl I know."

The men took off, and Jeremy's mother disappeared into her part of the attic to paint.

"You're not even trying," Jeremy accused Lynette.

"I'm as nice as I know how to be," Lynette said stubbornly.

"Not true. You don't talk to him the way you do to me. He doesn't even know you can talk."

She looked up at him, then away, so that he only got a glimpse of the hurt squinting in her eyes.

"Lynette, you don't understand." He was going to break down and tell her about the orphan asylum, but she ran upstairs and closed the door to her room; and he, without even a room to lock himself into, kicked the bench by the fireplace. Then, because that did not make a resounding enough thwack, he slammed the screen door behind him as he went out.

Two days passed with no headway made to install Lynette in Dave's affections as far as Jeremy could see. She passed like a shadow in and out among the adults. The only notice they took was of Jeremy, who was accused of acting strangely by both his mother and father. When the phone rang the third evening, Jeremy's mother called Lynette to answer it. Lynette came out of the kitchen after a few minutes during which Jeremy stewed, wondering who could be calling her. She looked happy. "My uncle would like to speak to you," she said to Dave.

"What uncle?" Dave asked.

"You know, Daddy's brother that Mommy and I went to visit after Daddy ran away."

Dave looked blank.

"He has the chickens on the ranch and all my cousins and the horses and the ponies," Lynette explained.

"Oh, the dude-ranch guy in New Mexico," Dave said.

"I was afraid of the ponies then, but I wouldn't be now."

"Go speak to the man, Dave," Jeremy's mother said. "Maybe—"

"He wants me to come and live with them," Lynette said.

"He told you that?" Lynette nodded. "And how would you feel about that?" Dave asked.

"Good. I liked my Aunt Susan. She says I can help with the new baby that's coming. And I liked Debbie. That's my only girl cousin."

"I don't understand how he even knew where to find Lynette!" Dave puzzled out loud.

"I wrote to them," Lynette said. "Mommy wrote for me last summer, but this year I wrote myself. I asked him if I could come."

The adults stared at Lynette as if they could not believe her. All of a sudden she had their complete attention. See how smart she is, Jeremy was thinking. They would not believe him when he tried to tell them.

"Well, if he's calling long distance—" Jeremy's mother reminded.

"Right!" Dave started for the phone.

Lynette took Jeremy's hand. "Let's go down to the beach," she said.

"O.K." Jeremy glanced at his parents, who still seemed to be moving in the slow motion of surprise. "Be back," he told them.

"Jeremy," Lynette said happily as they threaded the sandy path through the dune grass. "Isn't it nice?"

"Yeah."

"My uncle likes lots of children. He said he and Aunt Susan decided the more the merrier, and Debbie needs a sister because with all those boys around—well, they're not boys like you. They *hate* girls. At least—Jeremy, what's wrong?" She stopped short at the top of the path down the bare sea face of the dune.

"Nothing's wrong," Jeremy said, not at all sure why he felt so glum. "So that's what you asked the Glits for?"

"The Glits? No."

"You mean you weren't even *worried* your uncle might not want you when you wrote him?"

"Of course I was scared he wouldn't want me. That's why I never said about the letter. Because suppose he didn't want me—"

Jeremy shrugged. He felt peculiar. All summer he had been worrying about her and working to help her, and she had not needed him at all. He felt like a fool.

They both turned and stood staring down at the beach and out over the flat, poster-board evening sea so calm and dark beneath the milky sky.

"I think I'll go see Keith and Kevin tomorrow," he said. "You can find something for yourself to do, can't you?"

She nodded. "You're mad at me, aren't you?"

"No, I'm not."

"Yes, you are. My wish isn't going to come true."

He had never heard her voice sound so sad. "What do you mean? Your uncle said he wants you, didn't he?"

"That's not what I wished for."

"What then?"

"I wished that you would always be my friend. Like you were this summer, Jeremy, my best friend. I'm going to be your friend anyway, forever, even when I grow up bigger than you are now."

"Lynette, that was a dumb thing to wish."

"Why?"

"Why? Because. Because if you're going to live with your uncle in New Mexico, then probably we'll never even see each other again—never!" Now he knew why he felt so bad.

"I know that," Lynette said. "That's just why I wished—so the Glits would help us. They'll keep us friends. You said they're magic, didn't you?"

"Umm," he agreed.

"You can be friends with someone even if you never see them again so long as you don't ever forget them," she said.

He remembered how she dared to run into the ocean after him and how he was determined to save her no matter what. He'd never cared as much about another person. Selfish, just as his mother had said. But she did not call him selfish anymore. No, he most probably would never forget Lynette. Most probably he could not forget her even if he tried. "You're right," he said. "We will stay friends."

"Forever and ever."

"Well anyway until we're adults," he said. "Everything changes then."

"No," she said sure of herself. "Not everything."

He did not know what she had in mind, but it comforted him. And all at once it struck him that the magic of the Glits was real after all. It made him feel so good, really great in fact, better than he had felt all summer. "Let's run," he said.

He took Lynette's hand. They leaped down the steep slopes of the dune together sending waves of sand flying up from under their heels and screaming loud whoops of fizzy joy into the still evening air.